CYPHER
LORD OF THE FALLEN

More Warhammer 40,000 from Black Library

LEVIATHAN
Darius Hinks

GHAZGHKULL THRAKA: PROPHET OF THE WAAAGH!
Nate Crowley

HURON BLACKHEART: MASTER OF THE MAELSTROM
Mike Brooks

HELBRECHT: KNIGHT OF THE THRONE
Marc Collins

SHADOWSUN: THE PATIENT HUNTER
Phil Kelly

CYPHER: LORD OF THE FALLEN
John French

THE LION: SON OF THE FOREST
Mike Brooks

• AHRIMAN •
John French

BOOK 1: Exile
BOOK 2: Sorcerer
BOOK 3: Unchanged
BOOK 4: Eternal

KNIGHTS OF CALIBAN
Gav Thorpe
An omnibus featuring the novels *The Purging of Kadillus,
Angels of Darkness* and *Azrael*

LEGACY OF CALIBAN
Gav Thorpe
An omnibus featuring the novels *Ravenwing,
Master of Sanctity* and *The Unforgiven*

CYPHER

LORD OF THE FALLEN

JOHN FRENCH

BLACK LIBRARY

A BLACK LIBRARY PUBLICATION

First published in 2023.
This edition published in Great Britain in 2024 by
Black Library, Games Workshop Ltd., Willow Road,
Nottingham, NG7 2WS, UK.

Represented by: Games Workshop Limited – Irish branch,
Unit 3, Lower Liffey Street, Dublin 1,
D01 K199, Ireland.

10 9 8 7 6 5 4 3 2

Produced by Games Workshop in Nottingham.
Cover illustration by Jake Murray.

See Black Library on the internet at

blacklibrary.com

Find out more about Games Workshop
and the worlds of Warhammer at

games-workshop.com

Printed and bound in the UK.

For Chris Wraight and Gav Thorpe.

For more than a hundred centuries the Emperor
has sat immobile on the Golden Throne of Earth.
He is the Master of Mankind. By the might of His
inexhaustible armies a million worlds stand
against the dark.

Yet, He is a rotting carcass, the Carrion Lord of the
Imperium held in life by marvels from the Dark
Age of Technology and the thousand souls sacrificed
each day so that His may continue to burn.

To be a man in such times is to be one amongst
untold billions. It is to live in the cruellest and
most bloody regime imaginable. It is to suffer an
eternity of carnage and slaughter. It is to have cries
of anguish and sorrow drowned by the thirsting
laughter of dark gods.

This is a dark and terrible era where you will find
little comfort or hope. Forget the power of technology
and science. Forget the promise of progress and
advancement. Forget any notion of common
humanity or compassion.

There is no peace amongst the stars, for in the grim
darkness of the far future, there is only war.

'*The human soul cries out for simple truth: light and shadow, justice and sin, virtue and perfidy. In that simple division of all things, we find all the comfort of a dream that we are always waking from and finding a lie.*'

– Private writings of Malcador the Sigillite, suppressed and likely apocryphal

'*The following statement is true; the preceding statement is false.*'

– Ancient paradox

CONTEXT

Are you there? Are you listening? This is where we are going to begin. Down here in a dark place beneath the earth, a place of cold stone chains where the light of the sun is a forgotten idea, in a place where the only sound is that of two voices. Listen…

'Who are you?'

'I am no one. I am anyone.'

'No. You are… or were a warrior of the Legiones Astartes… certainly. You are a member of the First Legion, a Dark Angel… possibly. You are a traitor to the Imperium… potentially.'

'Yes.'

'And do you know who I am?'

'I know what you are.'

'Then you know that I am not here to ascertain if you are guilty or dangerous. You are both. I am the Warden of your incarceration. You shall never leave this cell. That is all that matters.'

'Why question me, then?'

'Because I want to know why you came here.'

'Destiny brought me here.'

'And those others that came with you, wearing armour as black as yours, what brought them?'

'Loyalty. Revenge. Guilt.'

'Do you have a name?'

'A name?'

'Names are the beginning of truth.'

'Cypher.'

'A word which means a code, or a person who is a non-entity. That is not a name at all.'

'It is the only truth I can tell... What of you? Is there a name you will give to me?'

'The first of my names is Hekkarron, Custodian Warden of the Shadowkeepers.'

'You do not worry at telling me that? Are names not power?'

'You have no freedom left in which to make use of it.'

'Perhaps. I can't tell you who I am, Custodian, but I can tell you something else.'

'What?'

'I can tell you a secret...'

ONE

Terra

The skies of Terra burn tonight. The false gods pour forth their wrath into the galaxy. Storms of lost dreams drag ships into the abyss between stars. Lights darken. Towers crumble. Horrors wake and walk the world. Screams and flames and panic. Guns fire on the battlements of Terra. The roots of the great Palace shake, and everywhere there is confusion. Everywhere there is Chaos.

In the Imperial Palace, warriors fight before gates that an enemy has not passed for ten thousand years. Things we name 'daemon' slither from the gaps between fire and shadow. Slaughter dances across the burnt earth. In the halls and chambers of the Emperor's domain, people huddle in the dark or walk amongst the ruin, weeping. No one knows what is happening, or how it will end. It is like the ancient days. It is a time of ending. It is a beginning.

Who am I? Ah, that question again. You know me, I am the one they call Cypher. And no, I shall give you no other name. This is not my story, though I am its voice.

And that story begins with me locked in the depths of Old Earth, beyond sight of all that passes in the world above. In the Dark Cells of the Adeptus Custodes, I wait for the door to my prison to open. The universe moves, it changes. What is true one second is false the next – I am dead; I am alive; I am bound; I am free; I am true; I am false. Everything you know now will be no more. Everything you have lost will return – all you have to do is wait… and while Terra burns, the first key that shall open the door of the future begins to turn.

High orbit

Above the Throneworld a ship lies still in the void. It is dark-hulled, a dart of metal the green of shadowed forests. It is called the *Absolution*, and it has come across the galaxy from the ruin of a war around a world called Fenris. It has come bearing warnings of an ancient enemy returned to the Imperium, of ruin and disaster. And it has arrived to find that catastrophe has outrun it. The enemy it brought warning of is not far away but everywhere: grinning from the night sky and capering in the flames lighting the surface of Terra.

From the viewport of a tower high on the ship's back, a warrior watches the fires glow across the nightside of Terra. He is called Mordachi, and he is an Epistolary of the Librarius of the Dark Angels Chapter of the Adeptus Astartes. He is a witch, a murderer of his kin, and in another life perhaps a good man. Not that it matters, but I like him as much as I pity him.

'What do you see, Brother Mordachi?'

The Librarian does not turn at the question or the sound of approaching footsteps. He knew the questioner and the question before they made a noise. An armoured figure stops beside him. This one is called Nariel.

'I see tragedy,' replies Mordachi, and he nods to the arc of the world crossing the view in front of him. 'You see that glow just beneath the polar circle, Nariel? That light is from the tower complex of Suun. It has stood since the days of the Great Wars of Heresy. In the most ancient records that exist, it is said that the towers persisted through the bombardment of the Warmaster and as Legions died at their feet. After that was done, after peace came again, the Lord Guilliman himself asked Master Mason Serena to raise the Towers of Suun higher. They endured the darkest of times, and now they burn.'

Nariel looks at the speck of light on the arc of the world below. Nothing stirs in his soul at the sight. After a long moment he speaks.

'There is a matter that has arisen.'

'What has happened?' asks Mordachi.

Nariel swallows. He holds the rank of sergeant. He has been a warrior for decades. He has moved through the circles of secrecy that the Dark Angels use to hide what they think is the truth. He has faced terror and doubt and not shaken. But in this second, he finds his throat dry. Can you blame him? I cannot.

'We have information, brother,' says Nariel. 'Ever since we were ordered to hold anchor at the orbital cordon, we have been performing our standard sweep and sift of all communications. Information security and coding has broken down in many of the units and divisions of the Adeptus Terra. There has been a lot of traffic, most of it incoherent and panicked, but the more we sift, the more we have been able to reconstruct.'

'What have we heard?'

'This.'

Nariel keys a control on his armour and a voice comes from the speaker units set into its collar. The words are scratched and spliced with distortion, but you can understand enough to feel them strike.

'It is he! It... Guilliman... primarch... He... returned. God-Emper... praised. Guilliman returned!'

The two Dark Angels listen as the recording unwinds into static.

'It is true?' asks Mordachi.

Nariel nods. 'We have large quantities of signal traffic that corroborate it. Secondary and tertiary analysis align – it is true. Roboute Guilliman lives.'

'On such days do legends walk...'

And now Nariel, faithful Nariel, pauses before he replies. He feels the weight of the second thing he must say, the name that will kill the spark of wonder in his brother's eyes.

'What is it, brother?' asks Mordachi.

'Amongst the data and signal churn this was heard...'

And Nariel keys his armour's vox-system again. The static chops. Sounds become broken words.

'Un...own...tes... C... her...'

'The signal serfs and cogitator wrights have reassembled it further,' says Nariel. His face is hard, emotion held under the skin by will. And Mordachi can feel it now. In his witch's soul, perhaps, he hears an echo of what he is about to learn. Nariel keys the recording again. More static, and then words.

'Unknown... Astartes...'

Rising from the chaos like ghosts.

'Cypher...'

And there it is, like a curse whispered into a king's ear.

Names have power as well as truth. And that name, my name, has the power to change Mordachi's future.

Silence follows as the recording cuts out.

'It relates to members of Lord Guilliman's retinue,' says Nariel, 'a group of Space Marines of unknown origin who were with him when they returned.'

'Where are they now?'

'The indications are that they were handed over to the Custodian Guard.'

For a moment Mordachi does not move. In front of him the fires burning on the face of Terra seem distant jewels. He can feel the blood in his flesh, and the beat of both hearts in his chest. In this moment, in this time stolen before he must speak, he can feel the balance of history waiting for what he will say next.

'They will take him to the Dark Cells,' he says.

'What are–'

'We are not the only ones who chain things in the dark from fear and shame, Nariel. The Dark Cells are the gaol and prison of the Imperial Palace. Every monster the Custodians cannot kill, or threat that they wish to learn from, they keep down there... in the dark beneath the Emperor's light.'

'How do you know of such things?'

'No secrets die, brother.'

Mordachi is not lying. But he is not telling the truth either. If I were in his place, neither would I. He turns from Nariel, and his hands go to rest on the balustrade before the iron-framed view of Terra. He knows what he has to do now – knows, and part of him wishes that the path was not so clear. Then he shakes the thought away, turns and begins to walk away from the viewport.

'Kill the serfs who have heard this,' he says to Nariel. 'Cleanse all of our records. Start a sweep of the orbital defences – full tactical assessment. Ready our brothers for war.'

The Dark Cells

Footsteps echo down corridors of stone as Hekkarron walks the maze of the Dark Cells. He walks alone. The quiet here is such that the purr of his armour and the fall of his feet seem to fill existence. His kind were made at the dawn of the Imperium, in the golden time of lies before the war between the Legions.

Those that know of the Custodians and the Space Marines sometimes think us kin. We are not, except in the most distant way. A Space Marine is a mutilated being, a human cut open and grafted with fragments of a demigod's essence. We are trained to belong to a group, to fight in a group, to think in a group. A Custodian is made by other means entirely. The mysteries of their transformation are not slotted into them like portions of meat but threaded through them as they grow from infants. It was said that all Custodians were once the offspring of defeated kings. If that was or is true, I do not know. But they are closer to princes than soldiers. They think alone, act alone, and fight alone. They are equally capable of the thoughts of scholars, the statecraft of diplomats, and the callousness of assassins. And here, down in the Dark Cells of the Imperial Palace, they are gaolers.

'Open vox-link to primary Warden control systems.' Hekkarron speaks the command and the vox-systems in his armour hear and obey.

'*Compliance…*' drones a servitor voice in reply. '*Authorising and processing auditory initiation… Access granted. The light of honour shines on you, Warden.*'

'Summarise Dark Cells confinement integrity.'

'*Compliance… Processing command… Dark Cells confinement integrity one hundred per cent on levels one through eighty-one. All is seen in the eye of the machine.*'

Hekkarron walks past the outer doors to cells and oubliettes. Some only he can see. Others bulge with locks and buzz with field envelopes. Behind these doors are things that the Custodians cannot or will not destroy. There is an old man whose words can kill billions. There is a coiling darkness that has no shape until it is seen. There is a small, black cube without hinge or lid, and on and on, locked and sealed from memory and sight. They are things from the depths of time and darkest reaches of the human soul. Some have names in the language of old myths: the Eater of Gods, the Serpent of Ending, the Unmaker of Thrones. Some have never been named and shall never be. There are living things, and machines and objects that sit silent and unmoving. And all are awake.

How do I know this? You don't become a mystery without learning a few secrets.

'Summarise warp stability and interface,' commands Hekkarron.

'*Etheric sensors indicate widespread fluctuation in warp currents, source external to complex. Null generators and etheric dampers compensating. Arcana wards and etheric seal integrity estimated at ninety-eight per cent.*'

'End vox-system interface.'

Hekkarron reaches a turn in the stone passage and pauses. He is counting, silently, each fraction of a second sliced off from the future with total precision. The Dark Cells are not a set of chambers, you see; they are a maze, forever remaking itself, filled with cut-outs and kill systems. Sometimes the Shadow Wardens let one of the lesser prisoners out to assess the systems. The result is never freedom. Hekkarron and his kind hold the totality of the maze in their minds. They move through it by synchronising with every twist, turn and alteration. If you could doubt that they were no longer human, this feat should put the matter beyond doubt.

Hekkarron reaches his count, and steps forwards. The passage behind reconfigures. Where there was air, there is now blank stone. His next step is up onto the wall as embedded gravgenerators change which way is up. The passage ahead spins. Traps and hidden weapon clusters fire at random and rearm. Hekkarron keeps walking, untouched and unimpeded, meshing into the lethal mechanisms.

There are few Warden Custodians in the cells tonight. Most have answered the call to stand in battle outside the walls. Hekkarron has remained to stand watch over the incarcerated. He is alone and even though he is a creature of near-perfect control, perhaps a part of him can't help but wonder if something is about to happen. There have been incidents before – no prison is perfect – and tonight the inmates and prisoners are restive. Hekkarron can feel them stir. Even through the energy fields, void locks, metal and stone he can feel them. All of them are quiet. And Hekkarron walks on, spear in hand, silence following at his side.

TWO

The Imperial Palace

The Imperial Palace... the centre of all, holy-of-holies for those that call their tyrant a god. The weight of the name alone is enough to drag a mind down into dreams of golden towers and radiant shrines. There are imagists on Gathalamor that labour their entire lives producing icons and pictures for pilgrims. Under their hands and eyes, the Imperial Palace glows with the light of revelation. Towers of white marble rise above avenues where the devoted weep as they process towards the gilded dome at the heart of the Inner Sanctum. Their clothes are bright. Carmine and palatinate robes ripple in heavy folds. A priest strides at the head of a flock of the faithful, mouth open in exultation. The face of a woman turns to the observer, eyes wide, hand pointing to the golden distance. A child rises into the air, claimed by cherubs to serve at the foot of the Golden Throne. An old man falls, hands raised in prayer, his tears bright as jewels as they fall. The noble aspect of an Adeptus Astartes warrior looks over the crowd, gaze watchful, haloed by rayed light. Eagles turn in a sapphire sky. On and on such images materialise from the hands of the image-crafters.

The pilgrims that come to Gathalamor pay for the images, the cost of a week's meals for the smallest and crudest, a noble's fortune for the largest and most lavish. They gaze at them for hours, imagining that one day they will see the wonder captured in paint and jewel and gilt. They clutch the images close as they breathe their last. They pass them to their children with words of hope. They do this not just with pictures but with stories and hopes and prayers. Across the Imperium it is the same, even if they do not have a painting from the Gathalamor imagists to gaze at. The Palace is a dream, you see, a bright and shining dream that gleams in the eyes of people whose lives are made of small miseries. It is a place where all is made right, and all the ills of life fade under the light of wonder.

The reality is not the dream. The Palace is a scab on the face of the wounded skin of Terra. From the zones of the Nexus Administrata to the Victoris Absolute, it is a tangle of structures layered on top of each other by time. Ten millennia have passed since it was built. Even then its stones were not set on barren ground. There were towers and fortresses here even in the time of Old Night. Those structures were made with the bones of cities. Those cities grew in times so ancient that they do not have a name. The Palace was grafted onto that older stock and grew from it.

Ages of history have passed since the Palace rose. It has been reduced to rubble, rebuilt, and rebuilt again. Its boundaries have swollen and retreated like the shore of a lake. Each time has piled its own filth on the past. Landing platforms sprout from towering ports like fungus on the trunk of a tree. Within a thousand years the platforms are the supports for hab-blocks given to Solar cults who gaze at the weak light of the sun through telescopes until they are blind. Wars between administrative departments burn regions down to ashes and rubble. New saints and heroes rise, their statues set to gaze at the Sanctum Imperialis. Centuries pass and their names mean nothing. The statues become the roosts of vox-aerials and sheen-birds. On and on it goes, changing through time, a carcass that the carrion-eaters never finish feeding on.

It is as vast as it is old. As I come to it this night, the Imperial Palace is the size of the greatest of ancient kingdoms. At its narrowest point it is hundreds of miles across. That is if you can decide where it ends and the giga-sprawl of habs and other regions begin. Yes, there are mountains bounding it to the north and south, but even those are riddled with tunnels and caverns. The Northern Zone, where the Dark Cells lie, is over two and a half thousand square miles, and that is just two of its dimensions. The Palace exists not as a flat structure but as a mass that extends up and downwards. Spires claw the bellies of polluted clouds, while their roots rest on crushed layers of structures that are over a mile deep. There are underworlds beneath the Palace. Warrens where the only light comes from fungi, streets as quiet as they were when the last foot trod them millennia ago, caverns filled with water that glows with chemicals and in whose depths still-deeper cities swim. It's all there, the past crushed beneath the weight of the present.

Billions live in the Palace bounds. They live as scribes, crammed into hab-units, scratching out words they don't understand on parchment that will rot before it is read. There are clans who fight for the right to light the candles in a single shrine. There are sin-bearer cartels who do penance for the misdeeds of others, and whose leaders clink with chains of gold coin as they walk. Great lords of Administratum divisions spend the decades of their careers in political battle to enact a single policy change. Inquisitors stalk the high and low places, searching for heresy and power. Far below their feet there are people who eat corpse fungus, drink the toxic waters that seep from above, and call out song-words that echo across lightless pools. Neither they nor generations before them even know that the sun exists. And these are but a few of the souls who make the Palace their home.

All of it, buildings, flesh and idea, resonates with the power that sits at its centre. The Emperor is the most powerful psyker to ever have existed. The Golden Throne on which He sits channels the power of thousands of psykers every minute. It annihilates them as it does this. Literally. They become dust and a ghost-shriek that joins a cacophony that drains into the Throne and into the Emperor Himself. Power poured onto power, until the immaterium beyond is burning and that pyre light reaches to the edge of existence.

Do you understand that? The Imperial Palace is more than just a structure, more than an idea: it is the centre of an inferno in the warp. And that inferno bleeds into the physical Palace and the minds of those in it. Two hundred years ago, on the Way of Ten Thousand Saints, images of angels appeared above the pilgrim throng. Eight out of every ten who saw the sight combusted. Days ago, a dying woman closed her eyes and then leaped up screaming. All those around her fell back blinded. The woman fled, alive, and shouting that the stars were gods. It was not abnormal enough to be noted. Here the miraculous and inexplicable are constant: chronometers wind through years in seconds and then collapse into rust.

Water freezes in pans over fires. The dead whisper in dreams. Idea, reality and soul all meet here. Just as we do, you and I.

I could go on, but I will not. I am telling you this only for context. You need to appreciate the dimensions of the Palace: in space, in time, and in the minds of humanity. It is vast beyond vast. These events are happening within its bounds. That makes it tempting to think that those events happen in a small space; that someone would notice what occurs; that the death and suffering, revelation and mayhem would register. They do not. The Palace is a world within a world. It is the Imperium concentrated down to its essence, like the matter compressed into darkness at the heart of a black hole. It is blind, ignorant and hungry. It eats knowledge, understanding and people. Set foot in the Imperial Palace and the cracks between mega-structures will drag you into the darkness. The shuffling of parchment and click of data will sift your life into dust. Here no one is anything, and everyone will be forgotten.

Well… almost everyone.

Northern Zone

It is snowing on the northern reaches of the Imperial Palace. The poisons of forty thousand years of pollution lace each flake. The snow flashes to steam as it kisses the void shields that cover the bulk of the Palace. Fires burn within the domes of energy. Clusters of old towers and districts the size of towns have fallen to riot and flame. Arbitrators and regiments of the Astra Militarum have sealed most of them off, but the situation is getting worse, not better. A lot of people have died already, and more will die in the hours to come. A lot more.

Above the shield domes, light flashes bright as missiles and aircraft explode. Those that are dying in those splashes of light are flying cargo shuttles, junk lighters and freighters. They are hoping that if they can reach the Palace then they will be safe. Foolishness, but that is the nature of human beings; desperation can undo sense in any soul. The interceptor squadrons do their work. Some of the craft get through, and then the defence turrets tear them from the sky. A few survive, but they never imagined what they would do if they got this far. They crash amongst the tangle of towers and burning buildings. Fresh fires leap up.

When the Dark Angels begin their descent from orbit, no one notices four more motes in the night sky. There are two gunships, small and hunch-winged. This pair carry the payload of the mission in their bellies: sixteen Dark Angels, their weapons blessed and their oaths made. Beside them fly two black-framed jet fighters. Together these four craft have slipped through the security cordon of Terra's orbital defences. Such a feat would normally be impossible, but the guardians of the Throneworld are occupied, the defences fractured. Even with that advantage, it has taken the pilots to the edge of their skill to get this far. They have danced through the fire-grids, scattered sensor decoys in their wake, and flown in the shadows of scanner systems.

'Entering deployment sphere. Terminal burn,' calls the pilot of the lead gunship into the vox. The four craft fire their engines one last time. Long cones of blue fire score into the dark, as they stab down through the atmosphere to their target zone. 'Initiate eclipse protocols.'

Then they cut their engines. All but the most basic pilot systems disable. For now, they are not flying but falling, four shards of metal following the pull of Mother Earth. Re-entry fire enfolds their skin. To anyone looking up with human or machine eyes, they are just four more pieces of debris falling from the night sky as stars.

Inside the hull of the lead gunship, Mordachi is reciting litanies of forgiveness in his mind.

'By my sword shall I earn absolution…' Even as the words quiet his mind, he finds himself thinking that this is a strange way to return to the world of his re-birth. 'By my absolution shall honour be reborn…'

'Entering primary threat zone,' comes the pilot's voice across the vox, quiet now as though hushed along with the gunship's engines. *'Target in sight.'*

Mordachi watches his brothers through the twilight sight of his helm senses. There are five. All are veterans and members of the Inner Circle; they are Deathwing. They know the secret of their birth Legion. For this mission they do not wear the bone Terminator armour of their office, but dark green armour scraped of emblems and marks of honour. Robed in hessian, their heads bowed over their weapons, they seem more penitents than fated warriors. A part of Mordachi cannot help but think that is as it should be. At the edge of his mind, he can hear their thoughts. They know no fear, but in all of them he hears something worse. He hears shame.

'Approaching target,' calls the lead pilot. *'The moment is at hand.'*

The distance between that future and the present is narrowing with every heartbeat of time. The Palace and its enclosure of void shields is beneath them now, spread out and glittering. At this speed they will strike the shield envelope like a macro shell. They will become flashes of light smeared across the air.

'All craft, light engines! Full burn!'

Thrusters and jets fire. The gunships and jet fighters slam level from their dive. The g-force that punches through Mordachi would kill a human. He blacks out. For a sliver of time he is neither of the world nor separated from it.

He is floating… body and mind in free fall…

A sound of countless voices vanishing into a storm-wind fills his skull. It's coming from the world beneath him. Reaching up to pull him into its embrace. To annihilate him.

Golden Throne…

A mind strong enough to light the galaxy…

A life that eats the souls of the living…

The world returns. The Dark Angels craft are skimming the skin of the Palace's void shields. Exotic technology scatters a cloak of lies into any auspex looking their way. The void shields covering the Palace form a pattern of overlapping domes of energy, each almost a mile wide. Nothing travelling faster than a thrown stone can pass through the shields.

'Incision point identified,' comes the voice of one of the jet-fighter pilots. *'Bearing zero-nine-one. All units, alter and match course.'*

The Dark Angels craft accelerate. They are aiming for a point where a dying cargo-tug is falling to earth. The tug is three hundred yards of burning metal, its thrusters fighting to push it back into the sky. As the Dark Angels close, a missile from a defence battery spears into the tug. Fire blows out from its flank in a great bubble. The vessel rolls and falls, shedding debris. The four Dark Angels craft are in its shadow. Their fuselages ring as shards of burning metal strike their wings. The tug hits the void-shield dome. A groaning boom shivers the night. Lightning crackles out. Layers of shields collapse like burst soap bubbles. The wreckage ploughs on down towards the Palace. Thunder rolls as the void shields reignite and collapse again.

'All craft, sword-tip formation, maximum speed and dive.'

The Dark Angels craft spiral into a tight group and plunge down in the dying tug's wake. They are so close that the pilots can see the glow of each other's instrument panels. Chunks of the tug's fuselage fly past. Blast waves from the collapsing void shields break over the craft. In the dark of the lead gunship's troop compartment, Mordachi still cannot shake the sound of distant voices ringing at the edge of his thoughts.

And then the four craft are through the shield dome. They track the wreckage of the tug as it falls and peel off just before it punches into a building and sends a plume of debris into the night sky.

'Landing zone in sight. Priority targets locked. Weapons launch at your command, Brother-Librarian.'

'Proceed,' replies Mordachi.

Missiles loose from the wings of the jet fighters. They have their targets: defence turrets, sensor towers and communications antennae. Amidst the fires already burning across the Palace, these are just a few more pinpricks of destruction. It is enough, though, to create a blind spot in the Palace's auspex coverage, narrow but sufficient.

The four craft weave between the towers and statues of saints. This is an expression of the skill of their pilots, like the cuts of master swordsmen. They are exceptional. There might be rivals amongst the White Scars and Raven Guard, but they are few. They are dancing with thrust and glide, balancing and turning on wing tips as spire tops flash past.

They do not see the missile array. Nestled into the base of a drum tower, the array's autonomous auspex sees one of the jet fighters, and launches. The pilot does not even have time to react before the missile tears half a wing from his craft. The jet fighter begins to spin, burning down into the canyons between cathedrals and towers.

'This is Nephilim Alpha...' The voice of the jet fighter's pilot is calm, precise. 'Critical damage sustained. Repeat, critical damage sustained. Flight control lost.'

Mordachi hears the pause that follows. He reaches his mind across the space between the gunship and the burning fighter.

+You know what must be done, brother,+ he says into the pilot's mind.

The pilot is a knight of the Ravenwing and knows that past this moment there can be no escape, no survival. His last act in service of his Chapter will be to ensure that no wreckage of his craft remains to betray that they were ever here. In truth he did not think that he would die here. In some patch of sky above a battle against many enemies, perhaps, but not by his own hand above the Throneworld of the Imperium. The fact of it fills him with silence as the warning alarms scream in his ears. Mordachi feels the ghosts of those sensations. They feel like ice.

'For the Lion...' whispers the pilot to himself, then triggers the fuel and weapon overrides. The spinning jet fighter becomes a ball of white heat before it can hit the ground.

In his mind, Mordachi holds the dead pilot's last thought until it begins to dissolve into silence.

The remaining craft speed on. Ahead of them a bronze dome looms amongst the towers and spires.

'Breach point in sight.' The gunship pilot's voice is just as cold and level as before his squadron brother died. 'Firing.'

A volley of missiles looses from the three craft and rips into the shell of the dome. Plasma and lascannon fire follow, carving the wound wide even as stone and metal collapse.

'Brace!'

Two gunships shoot into the breach. Thrusters fire. In an instant they go from maximum speed to a near dead halt. The deceleration rips panels from their fuselages. The thruster-wash buckles joists inside the dome. The remaining jet fighter circles the dome once, watching for signs that they have been detected. There are none.

The three craft settle into the darkness inside the dome. As the thrusters shut down the only sound is the patter of small debris falling from the breach above. The dome is part of a deserted wing of the Palace. Once it covered an amphitheatre, but that use has long passed and the dust of centuries hangs in the air like a fog.

'*Auspex shows no signs of detection,*' says the lead gunship pilot.

In the troop compartment the Dark Angels do not move. Mordachi raises his head. His mind is flitting through the rooms and corridors of this part of the Palace, ghosting past dust-shrouded statues and through forgotten doors. He hears the confused thoughts of the few soldiers and factotums his mind touches. This part of the structure is all but deserted. He pulls his senses back in.

Pain is beginning to seep into his skull. Out there, through the stone and metal of the Palace, he can feel a vast presence pressing down on his mind. He knows it only too well, but it is far, far worse than he remembers. This is the Imperial Palace, the seat of the Emperor. And that means that Mordachi has just stepped into the shadow of the most powerful psyker that has ever existed. Out amongst the stars a Librarian of the Adeptus Astartes is a creature of terrifying abilities. Here, on this world, in this place, his mind is a candle flame guttering in the wind of an inferno.

'Are you alright, brother?' asks Nariel over the personal vox.

Golden Throne…

Mordachi forces his mouth to form words.

'Our route is clear for at least four miles. The Palace is…' He pauses, aware of the iron taste in his mouth. 'The Palace is in a state of confusion. It will not last. We must move.'

'By your will, brother,' replies Nariel and switches to the unit vox. 'All units deploy and proceed.'

The gunship hatches open and the Dark Angels flow out into the quiet gloom. Mordachi is with them, his sword drawn and in his hand. Once they are out, the ramps and hatches close. Weapon mounts on the gunships' fuselages begin to sweep the dark. In his mind and the fibre of his nerves, Mordachi can still feel the cry of the Golden Throne and the weight of the Emperor's presence, blazing in the warp like a sun in a desert sky.

THREE

The Dark Cells

I sit in the dark. They have not chained me. There is no need. This place has no need of chains. I am alone, unarmed and unarmoured unless you count a simple white robe. Even if I had my weapons and armour it would make little difference. Give me a plasma cannon and I could do no more than mark the stone walls of my cell. Even so, they have taken my pistols, my knife, my armour, and, yes, they have taken the sword. They have not drawn it. Not yet. Even down here in the silence and the endless night, I think I would know if they drew the blade from the scabbard.

The cell is a cube, wide and tall enough for me to stand and find the ceiling just beyond the reach of my fingers. The stone is basalt. It is old, heart stone of sacred Earth dug up and shaped into a perfectly smooth box. The door fits flush with the wall, leaving no mark or seam. It is held shut by locks that a normal human mind cannot understand. Air circulates through needle-fine holes in the walls and ceiling.

To either side of my chamber are the cells that hold my brothers. All were raised to be warriors of the First Legion when the Emperor and His primarchs walked and warred amongst the stars. All of them are ancient by the way time is normally counted. All are now counted traitors by the Dark Angels that inherited that name. Traitors and slaves to dark gods. Some are just that, and some are penitent souls. If you listen, you can hear some of them...

'I am Azkhar! Named the Bearer of Swords! Born of murdered Caliban! Do you hear me, traitors?'

Azkhar, poor Azkhar, speaks to the air, on and on, turning over the heat of his anger in his soul. At the back of his mind, he can still see the green shadows of lost Caliban and smell the smoke as that world burns.

'May redemption find us...'

In the next cell, Brother Korlael kneels, head bowed.

'May our deeds be true. May we be forgiven.'

He will speak the words of contrition without end. He has spoken them for centuries. He knows that his pleas are empty, that forgiveness is not in the nature of this universe, but he speaks them nonetheless.

'The sun grows dark and shall not rise...'

Bakhariel, long lost to the promises of false gods and the powers of the warp, speaks in nonsense and truth.

'Dark will be the land, red the edge, the songs of famine calling... Dance the delight of dying... Walk the twisting path. All is inevitable. The sun grows dark and shall not rise...'

No one hears him. No one hears any of them, not even Bakhariel's gods of the warp. These moments are phantoms drawn for you by me, smears of charcoal on parchment, line and shadow. I want you to know this, I want someone to know us.

We are Fallen, forgotten and shunned, the shame of our Chapter, a secret hidden from the Imperium. Eleven of us – eleven lost sons of the Lion and brothers of Luther, locked away for this, within the Palace of the Emperor who made us. There are more scattered through time and the stars, but here and now there are just a few.

Believe it or not, these chambers are not the most secure in the Dark Cells. They are mere holding pens. We are newly arrived. The Custodians do not know who or what we are. If they decide we are truly dangerous then the darker, deeper places wait for us. If they decide we are not worth the effort of confining, well… then we would meet a different end. But neither execution nor endless captivity awaits me or my brothers.

Why?

Because the universe is about to quake, and the door into the future is about to open.

Northern Zone

The Dark Angels hit the Northern Zone Third Strata Complex of Primary Service Coordination fifteen minutes after they enter the Palace. The complex is not heavily defended. Twenty guards from one of the regiments stationed in the Palace watch over it. Some are veterans of old wars; others are draftees from high-born families. All are slow. Even the veterans have gone to fat under the pressed tunics and polished brass of their uniforms. The complex they are guarding oversees the army of serfs and factotums who work in the Palace's northern reaches. Theirs are the hands that light the candles, that carry messages and carry water. They are vital and unimportant. The complex itself is a place of shuffling feet, of murmured orders and ancient, calcified routine. Piles of dockets accumulate in cages. Orders and information hiss through message tubes. Hundreds of scribes sit hunched over lecterns while clusters of pict-lenses slide overhead on rails. There is dust everywhere, shed by billions of tons of parchment. Those that work here know that this is their holy duty and that their tasks are the purpose of their existence.

The Dark Angels arrive in their midst like a thunderbolt. Doors blast off hinges. The guards try to react, and die in a roar of explosive gunfire. The supervisors and prime-overseers cower. Some try to run.

Then Mordachi steps through the broken doors. He does not like what he must do now, but that dislike only adds a brutal directness to what he does. Coils of ghost light crackle about his head. The fleeing serfs freeze, nerves and muscles overridden. You can hear the quiet now, the heartbeats and held breaths. Mordachi walks through the frozen humans. It is taking a great deal of willpower to keep all of them still. Frost rings his eyes inside his helmet.

'They sent a distress signal,' says Nariel, turning from the cracked screen of a cogitator console. 'If someone responds we do not have much time.'

Mordachi does not answer. His awareness is flicking from mind to mind amongst the serfs, slicing, searching. He is being quick, not kind. Blood is running from some of the serfs' eyes.

'This one,' says Mordachi. He has stopped beside a man in the grey and blue and gold of a prefect primus.

The man is, in a small way, an important person. He has tattoos of office in place of hair: rayed suns, sickle moons, inked stars. He has a family that he does not see and a daughter who will inherit his rank when she is old enough. When he left his quarters ten hours before, he forgot to take his prayer coins from the bowl by his bed. Now he is looking straight forwards, unable to move or close his eyes, as a giant in armour kneels before him. The giant's eyes are red in a faceplate of cobalt blue.

'Forgive me,' says Mordachi and places his fingers on the man's forehead. The touch is gentle, the ceramite digits cold. Mordachi stabs his mind into the man's consciousness. It is not clean. A smell of cooking meat and static fills the air. The man's sense of self and past burn away as Mordachi strips away everything that is not the information he needs.

'Auspex detecting movement in the local area,' Nariel calls from across the chamber. 'Brother, we must be gone.'

Mordachi does not move. The prefect primus is still alive. Just.

'Thank you,' says Mordachi, then stands. The corpse of the man drops to the floor, the few secrets that he never knew were secrets pulled from his mind into Mordachi's. 'He knew enough,' he says. 'The primary gates to the Dark Cells are north, two and a half miles. Security is likely to be extreme but can be disrupted. Most vulnerable point of entry is an air circulation passage that passes close to the upper levels. We can breach by melta charge once the power flow is interrupted.'

'And these others?'

Nariel does not need to gesture at the serfs and factotums still held by psychic bonds. Mordachi knows what his brother means and knows that there is only one response. He knows, too, that Nariel needs to hear the words from Mordachi's lips. It is part of the burden of what they are and what their secrets force them to do.

'They have seen us,' says Mordachi. 'They cannot live.'

Bolter fire echoes out. Dust clouds the air and falls onto the blood sliding across the floor. One of the Dark Angels arms and tosses an inferno grenade into the cages of parchment. A second later fire is roaring through the air.

Mordachi walks from the complex. The image of prayer coins lying forgotten in a bowl beside a bed fades slowly from his mind.

FOUR

The Dark Cells

The witch comes to Hekkarron in the guard chambers of the Dark Cells. She comes unannounced and unasked for. She is tall, dark-skinned and violet-eyed. A coat of black hangs from her shoulders, rings adorn each of her fingers. Nine spheres of obsidian circle her without cease. The scent of frost and incense hangs in the air about her. She is called Ancia and she carries the fingerbones of dead men in a pouch at her waist.

There are few who can come into the presence of a Custodian without them knowing. Once, long ago, the warriors of the Silent Sisterhood might have done so, but that bond is long broken. Now it is only the members of the Augurs of the Psykana Ordo Auxilia Custodes that hold such a privilege. They are called Doomscryers, readers of the future and diviners of the consequence of the past. While the Custodians guard the Emperor and the Palace, the Doomscryers watch for threats to both those things. They sift dreams, divine the future and lift truths from minds. They are powerful. Very powerful.

You see, even here, amongst the guardians of the Throne itself, the warp is present. Psykers will be the death of mankind, but they are what lets humanity survive even as it despises and fears them. I can empathise with them. Hypocrisy, it seems, is the one coin that never loses its value.

'A threat is emerging,' says Ancia, no preamble, no greeting or honorifics.

Hekkarron looks up from the manuscript he is studying. It is ancient, older perhaps than the Imperium itself. Ice flecks the frame that holds it. The walls of the guard chamber are lined with books and scrolls and objects of the lost past. The Custodians are not soldiers or guards, you see. They are scholars, diplomats and assassins, and many more things besides. They are the Emperor's Talons, elevated in every way, humanity tuned and refined to the point where it is no longer humanity at all.

'The Neverborn howl at the outer walls,' he says, 'and fires burn within. Blood stains the stars. Legends return, and strength dwindles. Threats, honoured augur, threats cover the ground and fall from the sky with the rain.'

She cocks her head, raises an eyebrow. 'I see that dreams of desolation have come with you.'

'We do not dream.'

'Everyone dreams, Warden, even if they dream when they are awake.'

Hekkarron shrugs with his gaze.

'Tell me of the threat you have seen, then tell me why you have come to me.'

Ancia half turns away and moves to look at a book lying open on a stone table at the side of the chamber. Hekkarron swallows the instinct to see this as irritating. The Doomscryers are a strange breed; their thoughts glide in realms of unmade futures where the shadows of human emotion and logic overlap. He has found that it makes their response to certain situations less than straightforward. News of a fundamental threat at this moment, while almost all of the Custodians are fighting inside or outside the Palace – surely this should be a moment of urgency, of immediate action? Instead, Ancia reaches down and turns the page of the book with long, delicate fingers.

'The forbidden memories of Goge Vandire,' she says. 'Copied in the time of the Redemption Crusade by a dying scribe here on Terra...' She lets out a breath, eyes flickering closed, as her fingers linger on the parchment. 'The scribe knew he was dying even as he illuminated these pages. I can feel his fear in the parchment and ink...'

Ancia takes her hand from the page, and looks around. The spheres of obsidian orbiting her change direction. Her gaze moves over the rest of the chamber, over the niches of books and scrolls, over the ancient remains of broken weapons in cabinets, over the reading lecterns and the candles burning on their suspensor discs.

'You live amongst grave goods, Warden Hekkarron. Skulls grinning from the past...'

'What warning do you bring, Ancia?' he asks levelly. He is a being of masterful patience, like a tiger waiting in the shadow beside a watering pool.

The witch closes her eyes. When she breathes out there is frost in her white breath.

'I see a point of division. A single choice, Warden, one decision that will cause the future to run down one channel or another. Here and now in this Palace there is an agent of utter ruin to all we are bound to protect…' She pauses, shivers. 'Or that same agent will be a herald of hope.'

'If it is a fundamental threat, a threat to the Principal, then this is a matter for the captain-general.'

The Principal, a term that the Custodians use for the Emperor when talking with outsiders.

'It… it is not clear enough. My seeing is disputed.'

'The other scryers think you are mistaken?'

'I am not mistaken. I can see the future splitting, but… there is a possibility of observer interference.'

'That by seeing and acting on what you see, you will bring it about – that you cause it by trying to stop it happening.'

'Yes, but equally, by not trying I may do the same.'

Hekkarron looks at Ancia for a long moment. They are not friends. His kind do not have friends – just duty and the skill to fulfil that duty. But he knows Ancia. Before he became a Shadow Warden it was her insight that guided his hand to undo a plot that could have damaged the Golden Throne itself. He does not trust her – like friendship, trust is absent from his world – but he respects her.

'Why have you brought this to me rather than one of the Companions?'

The Companions, the title borne by the Custodians whose direct responsibility is the security of the Emperor's person and immediate threats to Him.

'Because I believe that the futures I have seen relate to someone who is here in this gaol of monsters.'

'Each and every one of our charges might be a principal threat if free, but all of them remain contained.'

'This is not a simple matter of a person with a single intent or idea. This is an alignment, a confluence of events. The warp is screaming, surge tides and psychic storms break over us. Nightmares pour into the world. Futures rise and fade by the instant.'

'The Neverborn have come. An Exalted Prince of Ruin has manifested on Luna. The storm is drowning us already, and this gaol remains secure.'

'The storm breaking does not mean that it has passed. There are… things still waiting in the currents of its spite… waiting to be born…'

Her voice trails off, and she closes her eyes to hold back a surge of pain. For a second, Hekkarron sees how much it has cost her to come here: what defying her peers has done and will do, what holding her eyes open to the warp and the flow of foresight is doing to her. In that moment he decides to believe her. She is indirect, where his being is as direct as the point of a sword. He would prefer it if she had spoken plainly, but that is a preference that does not stop him understanding what she means: that a prisoner in his charge might pose a threat to the Emperor, and that prisoner might break free.

'How will it begin?'

Ancia shivers and opens her eyes. There is a smell of frost and iron in the air.

'I believe it already has.'

Adeptus Mechanicus Temple, Northern Imperial Palace

'*All units in position, Brother-Librarian,*' comes Nariel's voice, low on the vox. '*Awaiting your command.*'

'Acknowledged,' replies Mordachi. He raises his head to look at the site of his next act of treason. Power and Communication Relay Temple Beta-One-Alpha. It is suspended on the inside of a shaft that runs down into the old, dilapidated core of the Palace. Clinging to the shaft wall, it is a jagged tumour of metal and rockcrete, hung with creeper-like power cables. It was built by the tech-priests millennia ago, a temporary bridge between the Palace's energy conduits and this wing. Like most things not made to last, it has been here for thousands of years. And like most small parts in a vast system its importance is not seen.

'The sword is drawn.' Mordachi speaks the ritual words into the vox. Around him, the wind curling through the shaft murmurs against his armour. He has done many terrible things in service of his Chapter and its secrets, but he never thought he would be here. He forms the word on his tongue. 'Execute.'

Missiles shriek from launchers. The wall of the machine-temple collapses in a ripple of explosions. Debris cascades down the shaft. Fire pours into the breach from every angle.

'*Resistance rising, brother,*' says Nariel over the vox. '*Now is the time.*'

Mordachi can see five of his brothers running along a walkway above the ruined temple. The Mechanicus guard-servitors that survive the blast activate. Heavy bolters and conversion beams blast at half-seen targets. Chunks are torn off the shaft walls. Metal and stone flash to dust.

Mordachi grunts with effort as he pushes his mind outwards, thought and will leaping across the distance to tether the temple. He can feel the simplified thoughts of the gun-servitors – *seek target, fire, move, seek target*. In his mind's eye he can see the squad of five Dark Angels reach the end of the walkway above the temple and leap into the abyss. The servitors' eyes lock onto them. Guns come up. Targeting systems triangulate. Mordachi reaches into the servitors' minds with his thoughts. The nerve impulses to fire their weapons are about to trigger.

'*Brother!*' shouts Nariel in warning.

Mordachi closes his will like a fist.

The servitors' heads explode. Their guns fire in death spasms. Mordachi reaches his will down into the meat of their nervous systems and yanks the dead servitors' muscles. They lurch around, dragging their gunfire with them. Bullets and beams of energy explode through the tech-priests and other servitors in the chamber.

Five Dark Angels land on the upper roof of the temple, swing down through its breached wall, and open fire. The light of bolt-explosions ripple in the wound carved into the structure. Then it stops, sudden as a cry cut by a knife.

'*Resistance silenced,*' says Nariel, '*placing charges.*'

The squad who made the assault are already mag-locking explosive and melta charges to the supports tying the machine-temple to the shaft wall. Arming mechanisms flash live. Nariel is checking the bolt-mangled systems inside the temple. He finds a signal console flashing, the severed limb of a tech-adept still locked to the controls.

'*They sent an alert message before they died.*'

'It will be too late, and besides, Nariel, Terra is burning. There is no one to hear their warning.'

'*As you say, brother,*' says Nariel.

Mordachi watches as his brothers finish attaching the charges that will sever the temple from the shaft wall. With it will come the power conduits that it tended, torn out like veins ripped from a throat. Across a wide volume of the Palace, power will fail, crucial systems will go silent, and a path will open.

Etheric winds howl with ghost voices in Mordachi's head as he watches his brothers get clear. He shivers inside his armour. The psychic effort of using his powers lingers on him like a fever. The winds of the warp are billowing through the Palace with storm force, roaring loud enough to block out the shriek of souls vanishing into the Golden Throne. He swallows in a dry throat and feels the next word come to his lips. It is a small thing, but – more so even than the previous actions – it marks a step not along a path, but over an edge. From here there truly is no way back.

'Detonate,' says Mordachi.

FIVE

Small things. Tiny, tiny things, so small that they pass by without notice. A word, an oath, a sword, a strand of wire, a rivet in a door, a bullet in a gun – billions and billions of things too small to count or to notice. But small things can unmake anything. We live the consequences of small things...

Will you indulge me if I tell you something? It is a small story, not mine, but important all the same.

Three hundred years ago, a man lived in a labour-hive on Mars. The code that he bore in place of a name was UT413. He was born to the work of the Eternus Forge Complex. He spent the years of his life on one task repeated over and over again. He was one stage in the thousands of stages that create a device that switches electro-charge between a single input and two outputs. In the sacred creed of the machine, his blessed task was coded as 675-D and the blessed component code for the electro-switch he was making is Chi-Zeta-Delta-10.

The men and women that weld the wires into this machine piece do not know that this is what they are doing. To helot UT413 his labour was a pattern of movement: lift, cut, match weld, check, pray – again and again until it was like the beat of his slowly weakening heart. He repeated these steps, thousands upon thousands upon millions of times.

With time, he aged. His sight began to fail. His hands grew weaker. He was not important enough to have his digits replaced by augmetics. He worked harder to compensate for his weakening body, and so it began to fail faster. He worked harder still. He knew that if his productivity fell below the required threshold he would be sent to flesh reclamation, and his nervous system assessed for repurposing into servitor units. This fate would not be his, though, because one day, as the sparks rose from his welding torch, the arrhythmic pumping of his heart rose, drummed a last wild cascade of beats and stopped. In the last agony-filled seconds of his life, helot UT413's nerves tried to complete the task that he had lived his life performing.

Lift.

Cut.

Ma... Ma...t...ch...

Wel...

The overseers took UT413's body from the sacred assembly line. The component he was working on in his last instant passed onwards down the line. It was complete, or seemed so, and so it went to become part of something greater.

The Dark Cells

And now, here we are and the flow of time and fate carries us on into the eternal question of the now.

The Dark Cells are one of the most secure and guarded

places on Terra. The locks are all but unbreakable. The power to their guard systems has layers of redundancy and backups. When Mordachi's Dark Angels take out the communication and power conduits in Temple Beta-One-Alpha, secondary machine processes should divert power from other sources. Ancillary plasma generators should come online. The systems watching the approaches to the Dark Cells should blink for long enough for Mordachi to get closer. That is what he intends. That is what he imagines will happen. The loss of one node should not have greater consequences. But small things do not follow our will...

The power to the upper levels of the Dark Cells cuts out. Klaxons begin to wail. The machine-spirits monitoring the energy flow respond. Power is diverted. Plasma generators buried in the bedrock beneath the Dark Cells fire up to full output. Fresh power spikes through systems. A blessed pulse of electro floods a switch made over three centuries before by a man who died in its making. The flaw left by the moment of his death finally bears fruit.

Metal fuses. Wires melt. Power uncoils into cables. Plastek ignites. The surge of power rises, now a flood. Fire and lightning explode out through the power trunking, running faster than machine-spirits can divert and shut down. Backups fail. Surge limiters become molten slag. And just like that, the upper third of the Dark Cells have no power. Monitor systems, containment fields, lights, air circulation, all of it gasping on its last gulp of energy.

For a moment there is quiet, but it is not stillness. It is an inhalation before the scream.

You see, this is far from the only disaster to occur tonight. A warp storm unlike any seen in millennia is battering Terra. The Dark Cells have been an island in that storm surge, the layers of psy-null systems keeping the storm's touch outside their walls. That serenity has just changed.

Null fields gutter. And the storm-swollen tides of the warp flood in. Unnatural energies normally kept in careful balance in the cell complex burst out. There are wards and self-sustaining null generators, and all manner of countermeasures, but they are not enough, not tonight. This is an epochal storm.

The wards shatter. Ghost light screams through the complex. The maze of gravity generators and corridors grinds like a key trying to turn in a jammed lock.

In my cell I feel it as a tremble in the air. I open my eyes. I stand up. The future is here.

Hekkarron is running. Light screams around him. The passage into the Dark Cells complex trembles beneath his feet. Gravity changes direction; the wall to his right becomes the floor. He switches step and balance without pause. The remains of a door lies across his path. It was a disc of cold iron and adamantium, half a yard thick and closed by bolts that ran three feet into the walls. Its wreckage clings to the passage walls, metal peeled and smeared into stone.

He can see a shadow moving beyond the broken door, looming against the flame-light. The guardian spear in his hand ignites with a shriek of lightning. Its blade is a smooth arc of metal etched down to the atom with the secret names spoken in its forging. The rounds loaded into the gun worked into its haft are silver.

Gravity flicks up the ceiling as he leaps through the ruined door. The shadow turns to meet him. It does not have a name that a human mouth can speak. It does not have a shape, but it steals one from Hekkarron's mind as he sees it. Empty darkness becomes a skin of molten iron. Eyes of blue fire open in a face of bone. Machine arms spread wide. Claws rake sparks from the walls. Hekkarron feels the fluctuating gravity flick out of being as the thing reaches for him. It is not fast. In a sense it has not moved at all. It is just not where it was before, and where it is now is with its claws around Hekkarron's neck.

Hekkarron's armour screams as it begins to buckle. He kicks off the wall as it becomes the floor, twisting free. Lightning-wreathed spear blade meets burning iron. Light and dark reverse. The nameless thing recoils, its form boiling into a red cloud.

Hekkarron lands, and the spear is already coming up, already lunging as the thing takes another shape. It is huge now, a rolling mass of splintered stone and black ice. Hekkarron's blade punches through it, but it is splitting, dividing like smoke caught in a gust of wind. It blasts towards Hekkarron, wrapping around him, slicing, puncturing. The black and gold of his armour shrieks as razor edges score its surface.

Hekkarron feels the promise of annihilation and the hunger for freedom in the thing's touch. It is agony, but he makes no sound. For a moment he is falling, falling back through the memories of his life all the way back to before he could walk, when his only words to the world were an infant's cry as he was taken from the flames of his home. He lets the moment and the sensation pass. Then he shrugs.

Muscles and armour ripple in perfect harmony. The thing explodes from Hekkarron in a cloud of glass shards. Hekkarron's spear arcs through it. Matter is unmade. Lightning leaps through the thing as it fights to take a new shape. Hekkarron cuts and pulls a device from his belt. It is small, an icosahedron in black matter. The thing knows what it is, knows what it means.

It roars and flies at Hekkarron one last time. He throws

the black device. It unfolds through dimensions as it arcs to meet the creature. Light shears. Distances expand so that the passage seems to extend to infinity.

Then everything collapses inwards, and the creature folds and vanishes into nothing.

The black icosahedron falls to the passage floor.

Hekkarron is already running again as he scoops it up and plunges on down into the broken maze of the Dark Cells.

Azkhar is already free as I reach his cell. Fire is spreading down the corridor. It is green and orange, unnatural, coiling like weed in floodwater.

'You knew this would happen – didn't you?' snarls Azkhar at me for a greeting.

'I know nothing,' I reply. 'Get the others loose. We do not have much time.'

'I should have known,' he says, the anger in his soul clear in his voice.

Bakhariel is already free. We find him in the crater that was his cell. Blue fire clings to the torn metal and half-melted stone. He is standing there, swaying, the hessian robe the Custodians gave him spilling around him as though caught in a wind. Wisps of blue fire dance over his bare hands. His eyes are dark pits as he raises them to us. There is no recognition in them.

'No sun, but an eye, an eye that is within...' he says.

'Brother, it is us,' I say, and pause, not going any closer. 'Can you see us, Bakhariel?'

'Night and day, black sun, burning moon...'

'He is gone to the gods,' growls Azkhar. 'Leave him, we don't have the time.'

I do not move. 'Bakhariel, look at us,' I say, my voice level and calm. 'We are your brothers. We are here. Come back to us.'

He blinks, once, and shakes his head.

'Brothers…' he says. 'There were green forests in the lands of my birth, dark and deep, and beasts. Great men came hunting them. Great men, in metal clad… High towers… Rain… there was rain.'

'Yes,' I say, and nod. 'There was.'

'Rain falling on the forests…' And the darkness and distance in Bakhariel's eyes clear a little. The flames still circle his hands, but the abyss no longer clings to his gaze. 'The storm is here, brothers. It splits the night of the soul. The fires of the pyres rise… Time runs swift to its end.'

'And what better way to spend that time than making sure we had a madman with us…' says Azkhar.

'We are all brothers, Azkhar,' I say, keeping my gaze steady on Bakhariel. 'We must never forget that. In this universe there are few things that matter more.'

'If you ever believed that,' says Azkhar, 'then you truly are a fool.'

'Follow me,' I say, nodding calmly to Bakhariel, 'we must get the others free.'

'And find weapons and armour,' adds Azkhar. 'I feel as though I am naked in a hurricane.'

We move to the next cluster of cells then. A still-functioning guard servitor swings out of a niche, its shoulders and machine arms heavy with weaponry. Lightning wreathes its guns as it levels them at us. I do not move. I do not die here, I know. Blue flame explodes from inside the servitor. Energy cells and ammunition cook off. Its body rips apart, the debris burning to ash as it falls.

Bakhariel walks through the falling debris. His hands are

charred, but he seems to feel no pain. The blue fire dances in his eyes now.

'I am the storm's eye,' he is calling, 'and through me it sees all...'

Perhaps you are wondering why I call him brother? Why I think him worth saving when his soul burns with the dark light of Chaos? There are reasons, circles of reasons, endless reasons all orbiting a truth. Here is one reason: I am many things, but I am not a hypocrite.

We move on. Korlael is next to be freed. Bakhariel rips a breach in the cell door with a gesture that leaves frost in the air and a fever heat on our skin. Korlael bows his head to me as he steps from his cell. I know that in his mind he is adding this act to those that weigh him down in penance.

'How many are free?' he asks.

'Almost all,' I reply.

'Our weapons and armour?'

'They will not hold our equipment here,' I answer, 'but if they were sending it elsewhere, it will still be close. The wheels of Terra do not turn swiftly.'

'But our freedom will not last long if we tarry here,' adds Azkhar. 'This place is a prison of monsters. If we are free so are some of its other... guests. Do we even know a way out?'

I shake my head, once. 'Get the rest of our brothers free, Azkhar.'

He is about to argue, but then turns and begins to move down the row of cells. He is cursing me, and the chain of past fortune that brought him here. Poor Azkhar. A soul filled with such sharp pieces of anger is a tragic thing. I always wanted a different fate for him, but our fate is not for us to choose.

'What is our purpose now, brother?' asks Korlael. 'Do we flee again?'

Fleeing… forever fleeing, forever pursued.

'No, my brother,' I say. 'Not yet.'

Do you still believe what I am telling you? Do you still believe in coincidence? Really, even after everything I have said? This tale must all seem impossible, and yet there is more to come. This is not my story. I am the catalyst, yes, the agent of these moments. But they are not mine, no matter how neatly they fit.

And fit they do. I am loose from the greatest gaol on Terra, free but hunted twice over, free in the Palace of the Emperor of Mankind, free as the world burns. This is pandemonium. So much broken and burning, so many assumptions left withering to ashes while the firelight blinds us. It is all too easy to miss what is truly happening.

How can events overlap with each other just so?

A piece of statue falls from the high roof of a cathedral. A pilgrim walking beneath looks up just before it strikes and kills him. Two decades later to the day, the man's son stands in the same spot to light a votive candle for his dead father. He hears a noise and looks up. A piece of the same statue that fell on his father crushes his skull.

Impossible. Such things do not happen, or if they do there must be a reason, a guiding hand, a grand design into which the improbable must fit. We don't like the idea that we are just pieces of debris caught on the wind of chance. Even if we can accept chance, we certainly can't accept one coincidence followed by another. Luck and ill fortune should be balanced, should be reasonable. But nothing in this universe is reasonable. And as for whether there is a grand plan…

Well, you don't expect me to tell you, do you?

SIX

The Dark Cells

There are fewer ways out of the Dark Cells than you might imagine. The Imperial Palace is vast and sprawling, and riddled with ways in and out and through its defences. But the Dark Cells are different. The Shadowkeepers of the Custodian Guard know their business, and they keep the doors into their domain few and well guarded. There are the main gates, which lead from the Palace down into the gaol complex. There are the secret roads that run down into the depths of the planet's crust under the Dark Cells. And then there are a handful of other ways.

One of these other portals is the Door of Cogs. Like everything in the Imperium, the Dark Cells need the machines of the Adeptus Mechanicus to function. The Door of Cogs is the conduit by which their priests enter the complex. It is also not truly a door, but a tunnel that winds its way back towards the Mechanicus Ambassadorial Enclave in the Palace. The tunnel is twenty-two yards across. Mag-rails run down its walls, floor and roof. Gun-servitors and slaved weapons scan the space with targeters, gene-spoor sifters and ident-scanners. It is here that our weapons wait. The Custodians turned them over to the tech-priests to analyse and then dispose of. Luckily, the stasis crates have got no further than the outside section of the Door of Cogs.

We come through the inner door in a blast of blue fire. Liquified metal sprays out.

<Threat detected,> transmits one of the tech-priests. Their comrades turn from their tasks. Gun-servitors pivot. Weapons draw energy to fire. They were aware of the power failure in the gaol complex. They were on high alert, but they had not expected this.

Korlael is the first through the breach in the blast doors. In his hands he holds a broken spar of metal as tall as a mortal human. It is a poor substitute for a sword, but it is enough to kill with.

'For the Lion!' Korlael shouts as he reaches the first of the tech-priests. His first blow cuts a tech-priest from collar to sternum. Thin blood and thick oil spray out. The tech-priest shrieks their death in machine code. Azkhar is not far behind his brother. He has a crude shield of twisted metal in one hand and a length of broken piston in the other.

The gun-servitors are firing. Azkhar lets the hard rounds ring from the primitive shield. Splinters lacerate his shoulders. Blood streaks down surging muscle. He does not care. He is smiling, a ghoul grin in a face of old scars. If the priests' energy weapons had charged up in time to shoot, the shield would have vanished, and a killer's grin would have become a skull's grimace. But while Azkhar is bitter, angry and lost, he is also very fast.

He hits a battle-servitor an instant before its plasma guns are about to fire. The impact rocks it back on its tracks. Azkhar's crude maul slams down into its face. Shattered crystal falls from the servitor's eyes, as its metal skull buckles into what remains of its brain. Azkhar is turning, looking for his next enemy.

And in that instant, he would have died.

Azkhar is fast, but he has not seen the murder-cyborg charge at him from across the tunnel floor. It is spring-release fast, a spindle-legged thing with a blade and pistol. It slices for Azkhar. He has time to feel the buzz of its blade shake his eyes in their sockets as it is touches his skin.

The cut does not land.

I am there. I came through the breached door in the shadow of Korlael and Azkhar. I have no weapons yet. That does not matter.

The cyborg sees me. It has an instant in which even its half-machine mind must feel a note of fear or surprise. It has a blade attached to one arm, a pistol held in the metal hand of the other. My hands grip its blade arm and yank it around. Gears and servos shear. They say flesh is weak, and maybe that is true for some, but the Emperor made our flesh and it is strong. I slice the cyborg's own singing blade through its other arm. It jerks back on its spindle legs.

I catch its pistol as it falls from the stump of its hand. The gun is a flechette blaster. A deadly thing, but not a weapon of a Space Marine. No matter.

I fire a burst into the cyborg's body. The shells almost rip it in half. And then I am moving, killing, shooting. I bleed. I destroy. I feel the dark shadow that is my soul speak. The rest of my brothers, my Fallen kin without home or father, are with me, and we do what we were made for. With broken weapons, and hands and the strength of our nature, we destroy.

It does not take long. And when it is done Azkhar turns to look at me. Poor Azkhar, it will not be long for him. I am sorry for that.

'Weak scum!' he snarls and grinds his foot into the jellied matter of a servitor.

'Look to the weapons, brother,' I say. The others are bending over a set of metal crates stacked on a mag-rail truck. Korlael and one of the others are prising them open. Armour and equipment lie within. I see Korlael kiss the key on its chain that it is his duty and honour to keep. Around us warning lights blink red on fading powercells. Bodies, limbs and machine parts are heaped in wet, red drifts. Blood gurgles down the channel at the centre of the tunnel.

'It is here,' says Korlael. 'Weapons and armour. Everything.'

'Everything?' I ask.

Korlael realises what I am asking, turns to check. 'No,' he says. 'The sword... the sword is gone, lord.'

The sword... The sword that I have borne since the breaking of our Legion. The sword that sits at my back, never drawn. The sword that I can never put down. Not until the end.

'The sword is gone?' Azkhar laughs. 'You carried it all this way, all this time, and now you have lost it. The last reason any of us have for following you, gone, and us free in the heart of the Imperium.' He almost shivers with laughter.

I do not see Korlael draw his glaive from the weapon crate. Neither does Azkhar. But now it is there, lit with lightning in Korlael's hand. Azkhar does not move. But the laughter drains from his face. You see, Azkhar is fast, and a killer, but Korlael was deadly when Caliban broke, and the millennia have only sharpened that skill. Sometimes I wonder if I could have ever beaten him if it came to it.

'Laugh again, Azkhar,' says Korlael, 'and I will cut you so that you will carry the shame of the scar until you die.'

'Cut me would you, Korlael? Why not just kill me and complete the circle?'

'I do not wish to bear the penance of your ending, Azkhar, but if I must I will.'

'Very well...' Azkhar gives a bitter laugh. 'Very well, I would not like to see you more weighed down than you are already, brother. But where do you think he is going to lead us now?' He gestures at me as he speaks. 'Into another eternity of skulking in the dark? Aeons of languishing in the Eye until we are as lost as Bakhariel?'

'There is only one truth...' intones Bakhariel at the mention of his name. 'The truth of eternity, the truth of Annihilation...'

'If you, Korlael, if any of you think that we should take that path again, then you deserve the pain of your guilt.' Azkhar is not laughing now. In truth he was not laughing before. There is nothing in his world but pain and rage: at the Lion, at the Imperium, at me. 'We are the betrayed, and we are here, on the world that first bore us, at the heart of the Palace of the Emperor who betrayed our Legion. Never have we had such a chance to take our revenge.'

'I will not break my oaths a second time, Azkhar,' says Korlael. 'I follow the bearer of the sword. I will not go with you into further damnation.'

'Broken swords and old oaths and newer lies,' spits Azkhar. 'What are we here for if not vengeance? Death and suffering and the weeping of those who wronged us, that is our due. One sword in our hands or another, it makes no odds. You are a fool, Korlael, and twice the fool for believing he will bring you to redemption.' He gestures at me again.

'I follow where my lord leads me,' says Korlael.

'He is not a lord!' roars Azkhar in reply.

'Enough.'

They fall silent as my word sounds. All of the ten brothers that followed me here to Terra are looking at me. Bakhariel, his skin sheened with sweat from his sorcery. The Scouring Light, who has not spoken since Caliban burned. Aphkal, who long ago lost the light of hope and the comfort of hate. And the rest. All looking at me. All waiting to see what happens next and wondering whether to follow me or not. Some, perhaps, are hoping that Azkhar will brave Korlael's sword and strike me down. Does that lack of loyalty surprise you? It should not.

We are a divided Legion. I do not mean divided like the child Chapters that hunt us from shame. I mean within every part of ourselves. *The Fallen* our Unforgiven brothers call us, as though we are of one mind and purpose. But we Fallen are as broken as our swords and oaths. There are those amongst these ten who hunted me for centuries. There are some who wish for nothing more than to kneel before the Emperor and hear that they are forgiven. There are some who believe in gods and some who believe only in the emptiness that waits for us all. Divided, hating, judging each other and me, here they stand and watch and wait.

Bakhariel breaks the silence. Closing his eyes and tilting his head up. You can see his veins, black beneath his parchment skin.

'Two sides of the moon, one bloody and dark, one sharp and silver...'

'Arm and armour yourselves,' I say, 'all of you.' An instant of hesitation and then they obey. It is a hurried donning of plate and weapons, done without the ritual that should accompany knights readying for war. Such are the needs of haste.

'Where are we bound, lord?' asks Korlael.

'We go to reclaim the sword,' I reply.

'And then?' asks Azkhar.

I shrug. 'And then we go where that sword is needed.'

Astrina Proscribed Zone

Mordachi never gets close to the Dark Cells. He and his brothers are moving through the Astrina Proscribed Zone when the gunship finds them.

They are on the surface in a space between the edifice of the Ministerium Omniscient and the half-ruined Archive of Ages. This part of the surface has been designated a kill-zone for seven decades. The only things that live here now are the ragged gangs left over from those who survived the Departmento war that led to the death of the Prefect of the Archive and the deaths of at least half a million souls. Yes: here, within a hundred miles of the Inner Sanctum, such things happen. Why does it remain a death sentence to walk these places now? No reason is printed on the writ of judgement that the arbitrators carry when they patrol the zone. There could be any number of causes: that the prefect leading one side of the war was killed five times and did not die; that people on both sides of the war would wake from dreams of a great and empty city and talk of how they saw a corpse on a throne alone in the desolation; that the Dark Cells lie under its eastern border and despite all the wards, I am not the first to break free from its cells. All these could be the reason it is death to walk the streets of Astrina. Which is the true cause does not matter. No one knows the reason now nor cares. It is written and so it is.

Arbitrator executioner units patrol the skies here. They kill on sight, but most of them have been diverted to the riots and uprisings in other zones. Mordachi is lucky that of the three units one happens to bank around the side of a building as he and his brothers are crossing from it.

White light catches Nariel in the open. He dives aside, a second before a tongue of muzzle flame reaches down from the barrels of a rotor-cannon. Rounds chew into the flagstones. Nariel comes up from his dive in a crouch, bolter raised. He fires. Bolt-rounds streak up to the gunship and burst on its armour. It shakes in the air.

It is a tough beast. Slabs of armour cover its frame. Plasteel plates shield its cockpit. Its cannons feed from deep reservoirs in its gut. Rocket pods rise from its back and stud its belly. It carries only a gunner and a pilot. The clenched fist of the Adeptus Arbites is red on the pitted black of its skin. It has no purpose but to kill. As the first bolt-round hits its nose, the gunner grades the encounter as requiring prejudice-extremis. They trigger the launchers on the gunship's belly. The weapons are indiscriminate, designed to scatter their payload like seeds from a hand. The rockets shower down. They are a mixture of frag and inferno charges. Shrapnel and flame hide the ground and envelop Nariel.

The pilot pulls the gunship around. The gunner is scanning with auspex and dark-vision for targets. They have no idea what they are shooting at. They simply want to ensure that they have killed everything that might be on the ground. They do not realise that they are about to die. Mordachi and the rest of the Astartes are in cover. The gunship has not seen them. Its sensors are tuned to movement and body heat; they cannot see the cold armour of the Dark Angels. Mordachi ordered his brothers to stillness as soon as the gunship fired. He is silently cursing himself for not having sensed its approach. Now they must eliminate it and make sure that it does not identify them and transmit that information.

'Wait,' says Mordachi into the vox.

They wait as the liquid fire rolls across the flagstones and the shrapnel rings on their armour. Even Nariel is now still, watching the gunship move above him as the fire washes about him. He is unscathed, inviolate in the explosions. Mordachi readies his mind, waits another heartbeat, then reaches out with his mind and will.

The gunship is warded with null-matrices. Too many of the people who persist in this zone are psykers, and the arbitrators are prepared. Rogue psykers are not Librarians of the Adeptus Astartes, though. Mordachi's mind blows through the wards. The null-matrices overload and melt. Mordachi feels blood vessels around his eyes burst with the effort. His mind hits those of the pilot and the gunner. Their immediate thoughts crumple. He sees that they have yet to call the engagement in. He chokes off their voices and paralyses their limbs. It's brief and crude, but enough.

'Fire,' he says into the vox.

Bolts slam into the gunship again. They do not penetrate its armour, but without the pilot's control, they are enough to rock the gunship in the air. It pitches. Its thrusters hold it true for a second and then they flip it up. It rolls over and hits the still-burning ground. The thrusters are still firing, ploughing the fuselage across the paving slabs. Then it hits the wall of a building. The thrusters are still whining and shaking the fuselage when Mordachi and the Dark Angels reach it. They cannot risk that the pilot and gunner might survive. Mordachi rips the armour shields from the cockpit. The gunner is already dead, mashed by the impact. The pilot's legs are broken but they have a pistol in their hand. Mordachi bats it aside before it can fire and slams his fist into the pilot's head. The pilot slumps, their skull a cracked and bloody shell inside their helm. Mordachi slams his hand down on their crown, shattering vertebrae and ending any chance that the pilot is still alive.

'Unfortunate,' says Nariel, coming close. His penitent robes are charred scraps. Mordachi shakes his head. He is reflecting on his lapse that let this happen. They have lost time and risked discovery. Worse, he has a growing suspicion that even when they reach the Dark Cells they will not be able to breach them. This incident only serves to remind him of a lesson that he learnt long before he became a Dark Angel. The Imperial Palace forgives no weakness, no matter how slight. They are the Deathwing, they are Dark Angels... but this is Terra and it has eaten the designs of warmasters and despots. He is beginning to think that their quest might be both foolish and impossible. He should listen to that doubt... but fortune's greatest cruelty is to help the fool to take another step on their road.

The vox-system in the gunship cockpit is still functioning. It clatters and hisses as Mordachi is about to step away from the wreckage. He stops, turns back, then motions to a warrior called Egion, the signum specialist amongst his brothers. Egion stabs a cable into the vox-unit and connects the other end to the side of his helmet. Data-light flicks across his eyepieces as he unwinds the signal from the distortion. The rest of the Dark Angels wait, eyes watching the desolation beyond the flames. They do not have long. The arbitrators will know that one of their gunships is down. There will be other craft here in minutes. There is no risk of Mordachi and his brothers losing the fight. The risk is that someone realises there are Space Marines loose in the Palace that should not be there. At that point they would become hunted. At that point the chances of their identities being revealed grow, and the possibility of completing their hunt shrink. They need to be gone, and soon.

Mordachi watches the sky. To the east a stutter of fire backlights the skyline. He wonders if, at the dawn of the Imperium, someone like him stood close to here and looked up at the fire of battle lighting the same point of the sky.

'There is an alert signal,' says Egion, releasing the cable and turning from the vox. 'It's coded to a vox-link between the Custodians and arbitrators in this section of the Palace. There has been an escape from the Dark Cells. It does not specify what.'

'Cypher,' says Mordachi.

'It might not be,' says Nariel.

Mordachi does not explain further. He does not, because he can't. In that moment he is seized by certainty. It has no tangible basis but is immovable. It is as though the howl of the death-wind coheres to whisper truth to him, and then streams on, laughing.

'It is him,' he says.

'How can we find him?' asks Nariel. 'The Lord of the Fallen can vanish now and we cannot hunt him across Terra without being exposed.'

'He cannot get out of the Palace to the north,' replies Mordachi. 'The Indomitor Wall has always been the most secure and there is battle that way.'

'He has used war as a cloak before,' says Nariel.

'He will not risk it, and it is too obvious. No, he will try and get out of this section of the Palace.'

'He will be taking a significant risk,' says Nariel.

'That is his nature, but with risk he will also gain options. He can try and exit the Palace in any direction or go to ground and wait.'

'That seems little better for us than his passing over the northern wall.'

Mordachi is silent. He is sifting through the memories of the human he was, past experiences he never thought he would draw on.

'If he goes south, he will have to cross the Keldron Rift and there are few ways to do that and remain hidden.'

Nariel does not reply. He does not know what Mordachi is talking about, but he trusts the Librarian. As much as one of the Dark Angels can trust another.

Mordachi begins to move away from the wreck of the gunship, first at a walk, then a run. His brothers follow. He is insightful, and in this case his instinct and reasoning are correct. I do not know that, of course; I do not even know that he is here. I will soon though, because we are now heading to the first of the two times we shall meet.

SEVEN

The Dark Cells

The storm has passed in the Dark Cells. Hekkarron and his fellow Shadowkeepers have contained or slain most of the prisoners who broke their bonds. Amongst the ruin and the re-bound monsters who shall one day end the world, there are empty cells and broken shackles. Things have fled this gaol. Amongst those escapees are the Dark Cells' most recent and briefest guests – eleven warriors in old black armour, my brothers and I. Our absence weighs on Hekkarron more than any other part of the cascade of calamities that have happened tonight.

'What do you see?' he asks as he and the Doomscryer stand in my cell.

'Too much,' replies Ancia. 'I will have to… This place is swimming with echoes, Hekkarron. Oh… but the echoes are strong. I…'

She falls silent, eyes fluttering shut. Hekkarron waits as the spheres of obsidian orbit her. In his mind, his own thoughts and worries spin in their own circles. He heard Ancia's warning and he has the beginnings of a thought that is becoming a belief – a belief that she is right, and that the agent of ruin she glimpses in the future is me.

My breaking free would needle his pride if such feelings were important to him. They are not. What worries him is that a threat to all he defends has slipped his guard. You might think that he would be out in the Palace, running after me like a dog after a scent. But Hekkarron is not such a simple foe. He is merciless, ruthless and as careful as he is swift. He knows that the best way of hunting is to know where your quarry is running to. So, he has brought the Doomscryer, Ancia, to my empty cell.

Her eyes open. She shivers.

'What can you tell me?' he asks.

Ancia kneels to press her bare hands to the floor. Her powers are prodigious and subtle. As a Doomscryer many of those powers are focused on looking at what the warp can reveal of future events. There are endless prophets and soothsayers that claim to do the same. Some even tell the truth. A Doomscryer is not a fortune teller, though. They use intent and focus to burrow into the froth of foresight. They are not trying to look at all of future events, their vision is narrowed to where events relate to one living soul – that of the Emperor of Mankind. All of them are primaris-grade psykers. Their minds can pull matter apart, read the past from contact with an object, and rip thoughts from weak minds. That they consider such abilities incidental should tell you something of their capability.

The psychic wards and null-generators are functioning in

this part of the complex, but they have been disabled in this cell. For now, the warp has been allowed in. Ice forms on the spheres of stone orbiting the witch. Her face is twitching. Her whole body is vibrating. Pale ghost light fills her eyes.

'He sat here,' she says. 'He... he was waiting. I see... I see...'

'What do you see?'

'I will show you.'

Ancia raises her hands from the floor, and as she does she pulls images from the stone. They unfold in the air, translucent, shimmering. There I am, remade as a ghost, as I was only hours before, sitting, legs crossed, eyes closed. Behind me are other shapes, things that might have been my shadows, and beyond them the blurred images of a figure with a broken sword in its hand, a king on a throne, a knight asleep on a bed of stone, on and on in a shifting parade. All of them are indistinct, as though they are not of this place but far away and blurred by distance in time. They change as Hekkarron watches, one dissolving, another appearing.

'What are these?' he asks. 'These images are not of events that took place here. Are they his thoughts?'

'No. These are unborn destinies. I have never seen anything exactly like this. It is as though his future is both clear and ever-changing. Some of these things wait in his future, but which of them is likely to occur changes with every instant that passes.'

'Are not all futures like that? One choice opens the door to one path and closes another? That was an insight of the quantum-scholars far back in the history of the species.'

'Yes, but this is not a branching of consequences. Look again...'

And Hekkarron looks, and his mind and eyes, so keen and sharp, see then what a glance missed.

'These are complete and different futures, as though what is to happen remains possible, as though the branches of the future do not collapse but remain. He is not following a path – he is following several. He is carrying the future with him.'

'For now,' Ancia says. 'At some point they must collapse and leave one truth.' She shudders then, and the ghost images flicker and vanish too. She takes her hands from the floor. They are white with frost. Control is etched on her face in deep lines, but her head does not bow. She stands. The ice begins to disappear from both floor and walls. 'The threat I see revolves around here, it began here...'

'Do all of these futures threaten the Principal?'

'I do not know.'

'Where is he going? Can you see that?'

'Not where, but I can see what was uppermost in his mind when he was here.' An image unfolds into the air. It hangs there, turning, flickering, betraying me by showing itself to these two.

'A sword...' says Hekkarron.

'It filled his mind. He seeks it like a father that seeks his child...'

'He bore a sword when he was taken. A great blade ill-fitting even for one of his stature. A rare and strange thing, that much could be told even without drawing it from the sheath.'

'Where was it taken?' asks Ancia.

'To somewhere safe.'

'Then we had best get it, Warden Hekkarron.'

'Why?'

'Because you may not be able to find him in the labyrinth of this Palace, but if you hold that sword in your hand, you will not need to – he shall find you.'

* * *

Ah, yes… the sword. Not my sword, even though I have borne it for many lifetimes. It is a singular weapon, made for one purpose, but now it has another destiny. You wonder, perhaps, why I had not mentioned it before? I will not apologise. We all have secrets to keep, and this is not my story, though it is mine to tell. So only now does the sword become part of events. Let us talk for a moment about it.

There are as many questions about the sword as about its bearer. Speculations. Theories. Fears. Here are the truths again. I carry a sword. I bear it on my back, because from tip to pommel it is as tall as me. It is sheathed. Its pommel is pointed and hollow, made to smash through a faceplate or bone, the metal scooped out to give it balance. The cross guard is an alloy of gold and adamant. Wings of red unfold across each tine behind an ivory skull. It is distinctive… Those are the truths, things that you can verify with your own eyes and hands.

The blade? To talk about the blade, it would have to leave its sheath, and there ends the truth. I have never drawn the sword. Or no one has seen me do so. If I have drawn it, and looked at it – *a long tongue of metal, sharpness spreading down both edges form the point, the fuller running down its centre* – and no one else knew, would I have drawn it? Is a man who falls dead alone and unremembered dead or alive? Perhaps both?

Do you think I have drawn it? Does it matter? Of course it does. Everything matters. Every detail. Do you think it would matter if when it was drawn it was not the double-edged sword of a knight, but a blade with only one edge – *one edge running in polished silver up the side of a scorched metal, dark and matt as moonless night, sigils cut into the black, glowing with death's promise* – made for a sorcerer? Would that change things? I think you know it would.

The blade is broken. That is another story swapped amongst

my followers and hunters. The Fallen and the Unforgiven. When I talk about speculations and stories, I am talking about them. Who else besides them knows that I even exist? Who else cares? Now there is a question. A broken blade, once whole, broken by war, yearning to be reforged... A metaphor for the two parts of the Dark Angels Legion: those that fell and those that stayed true. Two halves united again to great purpose. Yes... that's a story to follow into the dark. Is it true? Yes. All stories like this are true, even when they are lies.

Which brings us to the question of whose sword it was... Not mine. I think we can all agree on that. There are... possibilities, and with those possibilities come implications.

My gene-father, Lion El'Jonson, bore a sword. In truth he carried several over the time he fought beside us. Some he favoured for certain styles of combat, others for their symbolism. I once saw him break a battle line wielding mace and shield. The idea that a primarch might wear the same armour and carry the same weapon for hundreds of years, across thousands of battle fields, is laughable. That he carried many weapons, though, is not the point. When I say that he bore a sword, I mean only one: the Lion Sword. Pale fire in its heart, its passing the sigh of a last breath. An executioner's sword. A king's sword. *That* sword. Is that the blade I bear? If it was, what would that mean? Do I want it to kill a man, or because of what it symbolises? Perhaps both...

Kneel before the Emperor. Raise the sword to Him. Ask for forgiveness. Ask to be whole again.

Stand before the Emperor. Raise the sword point-down. Condemn Him for His crimes against mankind. Plunge the sword into the corpse.

The Lion Sword would suit both purposes, I think. But there are other possibilities.

For there to be betrayal and need for redemption, there must be someone who was the traitor and someone who was betrayed. What if the sword is not the blade of my gene-father, but the sword that was wielded to kill him? A tyrant-slayer. Echoing with power older than primarchs or Imperium. A death-dealer, a thing of hate and retribution. The Sword of Luther. The weapon of a man, not a demigod, a weapon made to kill gods and their spawn.

Or what if it is neither? What if it is not the blade that matters but what it can cut through, what it can open? The Unforgiven carry their Heavenfall Blades, and they are keys as well as weapons. All the secrets they have locked away in their fortress are opened by those blades. What if there was another of them? An unnamed sibling to those blades carried by the Masters and Grand Masters of the Dark Angels? A blade that could open the doors to one last secret that they do not even realise is there. It could be, couldn't it? What else would drive me to carry a sword I never use and keep it safe? What could be worth so much blood and suffering?

Surely, you know the answer already...

In this universe the only thing that has value is secrets.

EIGHT

Keldron Rift

While Hekkarron talks to Ancia, I am running with my brothers into the tangle of the Palace. We are armed and armoured, and gunfire still lingers in our ears. We reach the end of the tunnel we have followed for the last mile and find that its broken mouth hangs open on the side of a canyon between two fractured cliffs of stonework and rockcrete.

At some point in the last centuries, a shift of tectonic plates has split this section of the Palace and left an abyss running through it. A honeycomb of truncated rooms and corridors lines the cliff faces above, below and opposite us. Falls of liquid cascade down from upper levels. My eyes can see a scrap of what might be moonlight high above. We halt on the edge of the drop. Bridges span the gaps high above us, and you can see the lights of vehicles and people moving on them. Most of that traffic looks panicked. As we look up, I hear the chatter of distant gunfire. A line of rounds stitches the dark. Something explodes with a brief flash high above. This far away you can barely hear the thunder-crack of detonation.

'A wound in the body of the world that weeps for the fall of kingdoms,' murmurs Bakhariel, looking down into the canyon.

'Poetic, as ever,' sneers Azkhar, 'but it is also a problem if we don't want to go back the way we came. Did your plans not include a hole in the ground, Brother Cypher?'

'There is a bridge,' says Korlael. 'Look there, half a mile down. No traffic visible on it either.'

'That is because it is a ruin,' says Azkhar. He is right, the bridge Korlael is talking about is half a mile of rust and half-fraying suspension cables spanning the waiting drop. 'It might be better to try to fly than use that to cross.'

I consider the options for a moment. They are few. In the distance, wild gunfire chuckles.

'We take it,' I say.

My brothers say nothing, not even Azkhar. We begin to climb down the wall of the canyon towards the bridge. I do not see Nariel and Mordachi's eyes watching the bridge from the wall of the canyon opposite, but they are there.

'You are certain they will come this way?' asks Nariel.

'Nothing is certain,' replies Mordachi. 'But this is the most probable way they would come.'

'If they do, we could send them down to the dark with the first shots. That bridge is half-collapsed as it is. A few charges and a missile into the weak point and it falls.'

'We could, but that offers no possibility of redemption. Theirs or ours.'

The Dark Angels lapse back into silence. They wait above the chasm and watch the desolate bridge across the dark. Since they left the Astrina Proscribed Zone they have been sifting communications and Mordachi has been plundering every mind he can touch without being detected. They are good hunters. They have mapped the ground before we move into it and selected the place that they shall meet us.

'There is movement,' comes the voice of one of the Dark Angels across the vox, *'opposite side of the abyss, six hundred feet above the target bridge and moving downwards.'*

'Confirmed,' says Nariel. 'Stand by.'

We begin to cross the bridge. We go inch by inch, in pairs. I wait and watch. The spray of water falling from above forms a mist in the chasm. There is an itch under the skin of my scalp. I shift, flicking my gaze across the dark beyond the bridge.

'Is there something wrong, lord?' asks Korlael.

I do not answer him. Poor, loyal, guilty Korlael. He can feel it, too. There is something coming. I do not know what it is, none of us do, but we can feel it. We have survived being hunted for many lifetimes, and that has given us an instinct for caution. Why do we not stop or turn back? Because we are in a hurry, because instinct is sometimes wrong. Those are good reasons, don't you think? Of course, I might have a different reason. I might be lying. Ahead I see the first of our number reach the centre of the bridge. The old cables are creaking.

A pall of mist shifts across the bridge. I can hear the wind creaking the cables. High above, the gunfire of earlier has become quiet.

'Lord?' asks Korlael.

'It is time,' I say.

I begin to cross the bridge. Korlael is at my side. The dozens of keys that hang from his armour tap on the ceramite as he moves. We do not hurry. My weapons are not in my hands. Above the bridge, Mordachi sees me for the first time.

'That is him...' says Mordachi.

He cannot keep the awe from his voice. To those of the Inner Circle, I am more than a quarry. Time and elusiveness have grown the shadow of my existence in their minds. I am the aleph of their quest for redemption, the name and image that represents all they hate, and hope for, and fear.

'It is truly him, the Lord of the Fallen himself...'

'He is approaching the middle of the bridge,' says Nariel. 'The command is yours, Brother-Librarian.'

Mordachi's expression hardens around his gaze as he stares at me.

'Take him,' he says.

The first missile hits the bridge ten paces behind us. It rips through the metal cabling and walkway. Then bolter fire, and then a second later the sound of return fire, and the dark is strobing with explosions. The bridge twists and pitches sideways under our feet. The supports on one side snap. We are running, my brothers firing. The bridge screams as it twists. I can see figures moving on the cliff face ahead, figures in dark power armour and a figure with ghost light haloing his helm, a sword in his hand. He is poised to leap down onto the far end of the bridge. He is looking right at me...

In the instant I can feel the hate and the shock and the awe in that gaze.

They are here.

Against all chance they are here. The Dark Angels. The bitter sons of our father. And part of me sees and knows that of course this was inevitable. The future we are fated for is inexorable. We can try to outrun it. We can try to meet it early, we can try to turn aside from it, but it shall come for us just the same.

'For the Lion!' shouts Korlael. We are running forwards, all of us, Azkhar with his mace in his fist, bareheaded, snarling; Korlael's sword a flash of lightning-shrouded steel; Bakhariel, blue fire wreathing his open fists and burning from his eyes, and the rest, running across the bridge as it twists. I can see our hunters – they are across our path and on the canyon face above. Three of them are on the bridge, blades lit, guns firing… black armour and penitent robes, gun flash and blurred movement. And for a moment, seen in a blink, you would wonder which was which, the Fallen and the Unforgiven.

+Yield and you will have redemption!+ shouts Mordachi into our minds.

Redemption… such a promise. And they mean it, they truly do, but you cannot offer what is not yours to give.

I kill the first of Mordachi's warriors. Three shots. A bolt-round to tear his gun from his hands. A second into his chest to punch him backwards. A stream of plasma through his head as he rises. An instant for all three. The guns drawn and fired faster than the blink of time. And then there is a corpse falling. The first of Mordachi's brothers that I will kill but not the last.

Are you surprised? You shouldn't be. I am not an angel made for forgiveness.

The death of his brother stuns Mordachi for a second. He has hunted our kind before, but not me. His shock only lasts a moment, though. He pulls the currents of the warp in line with his thoughts and reaches for us.

Bonds of invisible energy wind over my limbs. A step behind

me, Korlael's charge falters as telekinetic cords wrap around him. Pale light and frost glitter in the air above the collapsing bridge. Mordachi's mind closes around our bodies. He is in agony, the screams in his mind razors and needle points. But we are held, and he will bear all the pain he needs to, to maintain that grip. He can hear the screams of souls vanishing into the Golden Throne and the shriek of the storm tide beyond.

'Sever… the… bridge…' he commands.

A missile shoots from the canyon wall. It strikes the bridge and cuts its last ties in a flash of fire. The bridge breaks and begins to fall. We stay where we are as the ground beneath us drops away. Mordachi's telekinetic will is keeping us from falling. To hold us is a strain that would break lesser men. But he is a strong soul, he could have held firm.

But then Bakhariel's mind crashes into Mordachi's like a mailed fist. My brother is alight with fire. His shape and armour are a black outline at the centre of a blinding inferno.

'Red is the blade's edge,' calls Bakhariel, 'and bright the burning sky!'

And with a tug of thought, he lifts the ruin of the bridge up from the abyss before it can fall. Blocks of stone and twisted girders rise up beneath us. Girders and cables twist into a road under our feet.

Mordachi reels, crying out in pain. My feet slam into the bridge as it rises. Snakes of pale light arc between the broken stone and metal. I am running. Korlael, Azkhar and the rest are with me. Bakhariel is rising into the air, a burning angel above the abyss.

Mordachi has fallen to one knee on the ledge above. He is bleeding inside his armour. He wanted to take us alive, to take us back to the places of interrogation and confession that lead to death and empty absolution. That is what he wanted, but if that cannot be, then he will do what he must. He will see that we do not go free.

'Open fire!' he shouts.

The Dark Angels on the canyon wall fire. Missiles, plasma and a deluge of bolt-rounds streak the dark. A missile tears apart Brother Khael as he reaches the end of the bridge. Scraps of flesh and shards of armour scatter into the dark. There is not enough left of him to scream as he falls. The fire pours down on us. Lines of rounds converge on Malchiel, and he vanishes. Another of our brothers gone, ripped on a rolling drumbeat of bolt impacts.

A round strikes my shoulder and explodes. My helmet rings with the kiss of shrapnel. I stumble, half falling on the stones of a bridge that is now only held together by threads of witch-craft. I am so close to the end. I can see the muzzles of guns and the fingers squeezing on triggers to send me down into the dark.

But I do not die this night.

Above us Bakhariel ascends, glowing like a fallen star shot back into the sky. He shivers. Shards of rubble rise to spin around him. The fire pouring from his cracked soul is blinding. He is luminous, and he is vile. How often has he been our salvation.

He shivers again and the cyclone rock shards fly forwards faster than sound. They strike armour, punch through eyepieces, hammer bodies to pulp. Korlael and Azkhar and I are at the end of the bridge now. I kill another two Dark Angels then, one for mercy, one for spite. And we are through their ambush, and halfway down the tunnel beyond. Azkhar pauses to fire into a warrior who is pulling himself to his feet. There are nine of us now. They could have killed more of us, but they wanted us alive. Such is the reward of pride. Mordachi and his remaining warriors are following us even as we run. Bakhariel is half floating, half stumbling with us. The warp fire wreathing him gutters. The passage behind us is starting to collapse.

Azkhar is still trailing, firing back at Mordachi and his warriors.

'Azkhar,' calls Korlael, 'enough!'

'You are a fool and a coward, Korlael!' answers Azkhar.

And as Azkhar half turns to spit his contempt at his brother, a wave of telekinetic force yanks him backwards as the passage closes between us and him with a roar of breaking stone.

Korlael turns and runs back, falling stone shattering from his pauldrons and helm as he looks for a way back through. The rest of us pause. One fewer now, just eight knights of Caliban on the road to absolution.

'Azkhar!' shouts Korlael at the rockfall.

'The gods have given us what grace they can,' gasps Bakhariel. He is trembling with psychic fatigue. 'This time is sand in our fingers. We must flee if we are to live.'

'Azkhar is our brother,' snarls Korlael. 'We swore an oath that we would keep each other from the Unforgiven.'

I sometimes wish we were all like Korlael – loyal, true to the last. But we are not.

'Azkhar is gone,' I say aloud, 'and we must leave.'

The patter of falling stones and debris fills the moment that follows. Korlael is looking at me, the eyes of his helm ember-red in the gloom.

'If that is your will, lord?' he asks.

'It is.'

And so we flee on.

NINE

The Court Of Assassins

Hekkarron moves through the Palace like the light of a sun cutting through the night. Fires burn in the grand wings and battle rattles its walls. Much of the grand structure belongs to mayhem and ruin. Yes, even inside the walls of the great and glorious seat of the Emperor, things fall apart. Such are the times. The places of order are islands in the oceans of panic and fire. Gates are barred, and guns and blades are set to cut down any who seek to pass through. Great worthies of Terra have already died by the hundred for seeking sanctuary in the sealed enclaves, but Hekkarron and Ancia pass through them all and neither blade nor word stops them. He is a guardian of this realm, one of the high agents of its protection and bearer of the authority of the Throne. You do not bar the path of a Custodian and a Doomscryer augur, and none do until they come to the threshold of the place they seek.

That place is set high on a tiered tower to the north of the Lion's Gate. It has no guards, but it has no need of them. Ice winds batter the tower and snow clings to the granite bridges that link it to the structure of the Palace around it. The windows and arrow slits are unglazed and the wind moans as it spirals through the insides. Above its spire, the sheen of void shields hazes the moonlight. Gunfire and the arc-flash of aerial combat stitch the dome of the sky. Crows perch on the grotesques that jut from the tower, and watch all that pass with red, bionic eyes. Like several of the structures within the bounds of the Palace, this place is an outpost of one of the organisations that keep the half-dead Imperium alive. It is called the Court of Assassins.

Ancia and Hekkarron pause on the bridge leading to the tower. A wind whistles over the exposed span of stone carrying snow and the kiss of ozone from the shields above.

'We are being watched,' says Ancia. She glances up as one of the cyber-crows launches from its perch and circles above them.

Hekkarron nods without looking away from the empty span of the bridge ahead. 'They have been observing us for the last six miles with at least ten cyber-ocular task units. A member of their Vindicare Clade has been watching us through the scope of his rifle since we stepped onto this bridge. The agents of the Officio Assassinorum are thorough.'

'There is another, too,' says Ancia, casually. 'A Callidus face changer who has tracked us since we crossed the Procession of Heroes.'

'Yes, that too.'

'They should be careful.'

'The Assassins have always been cautious. It is how they have endured.'

'I meant in this instance. I can feel the tide direction of the sniper's thoughts. They are worried, Hekkarron. And they are less in control of their fears than they think. And they are right to be afraid.'

'Why so?' he asks, though he knows the answer.

'Because if they try to stand in our way, we will kill them all, of course.'

They walk on across the snow-caked granite.

Does Ancia's sentiment surprise you? Does her confidence that the pair of them could kill the apex murderers of the Imperium seem misplaced? Perhaps. The Assassins are a part of the Imperium as old as the Custodians, older perhaps. They have killed people great and small, and there are few things that they cannot usher across the threshold of death given enough time. But just as the Assassins are near-perfect killers, so are the Custodians the truest bodyguards ever to bear that burden. Both breeds are gene-wrought and trained with methods that would kill even mighty warriors. Both are subtle, and quick and sharp, and lethal. One is a gilded demigod, the other a waiting shadow. Two sides of a coin, alike and yet not. So, perhaps Ancia is right in her confidence. Either way, a war between Assassins and Custodians is as unlikely as it would be devastating.

The entrance into the tower has no door, but a man stands across their path. He is wrapped in a tattered velvet cloak. A leather mask hides all but his mouth, and covers his eyes, so that he seems like one of the sightless pilgrims that crowd the holy-ways. He is not truly blind. His sightlessness is part of his ritual role in the court, but even with his eyes covered he knows every detail of the world around him. He leans on the haft of an axe taller than he is. He is old, and his flesh can no longer tolerate the polymorphine drug that once let him change his face and form. Old… but the slowness of his movements and the shiver in his crooked fingers are a lie. He is called Cradus and he is the Keeper of this Court of Assassins.

'You will stop there, Custodian,' he says.

Hekkarron stops. The wind stirs the red plume on his helm. Five human paces separate them.

'We come with urgent need, Honoured Keeper,' says Hekkarron.

'There is no honour here, Warden Hekkarron,' says Cradus. His lips crook into a rictus grin of yellow teeth. 'But I appreciate the courtesy. What do you and your augur want?'

'A weapon was sent to your keeping this night. A sword. You know of what I speak. You will return it to me.'

Cradus does not answer for a moment, but stands, the frost-marked velvet of his cloak flapping in the wind.

'Come within,' he says at last. 'This is a matter that will need discussion.' He turns and begins to limp through the open mouth of the door into the tower. After two steps he pauses and looks back, jerking his head at Ancia. 'The witch may wish to remain outside. The company may not be to her liking.'

'She will not be staying out here,' replies Ancia, and the scorn in her voice could shame a monarch. 'And if you don't address me directly and properly I will reach into your skull, rip your thoughts in half and leave you dribbling on the floor.'

Cradus chuckles. 'Good… Very good. My apologies, Honoured Augur Ancia, but the warning still stands. You may not like what waits within.'

Cradus turns without further formality and limps into the interior of the tower. Ancia glances at Hekkarron, and raises an eyebrow. The Warden offers the smallest of shrugs in return and follows the Assassin.

* * *

The inside of the tower is like the spiral of a seashell, cut from stone and filled with the shadows cast by burning torches. Frost hangs in the air after every breath. There are no windows. Flights of stairs curve up and away, meet, split and vanish into doorways without obvious sense or reason. The open space they enclose is a shallow bowl ten paces across with steps cut into the sides. At the centre is a circular opening that goes down into darkness. This is the Court of Assassins. It is said that it is made in the image of the Death Courts of Old Night, when the lowly and the powerful would come and offer and argue for the end of their enemies and the protection of those they cared for. Just like those dead empresses and kings of old, Hekkarron and Ancia are motioned to stand at the lowest point of the bowl, the circle of emptiness open at their feet.

'Please, stand here, Lord Warden and Lady Augur,' says Cradus the Keeper. 'You know the forms and customs I am sure, but we can never be too careful in matters of manners, can we?'

'As you wish...' replies Hekkarron. He and Ancia wait as Cradus limps to the other side of the bowl. Ancia begins to feel the cold then. Just a tremor in the deep flesh and bone at first, and then a rising touch of ice sharpening to thousands of needles inside her mind and body. It is nothing to do with the temperature in the chamber. It is the cold of a different type, deeper than the abyss of space, colder than dead stars. To her it is terrifying. She does not show it outwardly; except perhaps in the contracting of her pupils, and the stillness of her face.

'Something is coming...' she says, forcing calm into her voice.

Hekkarron can feel it too now, a numbing cold and note of

dread that even his ascended soul can sense. He knows what it is, too. Not a frost, nor the touch of witchery; this is the cold of nothingness, of the screaming oblivion that eats all hope and light and leaves nothing but night.

'The Observer and the Voice honour you with their presence,' says Cradus.

Two figures walk from the tangle of shadows at the chamber's edge. The first wears a mask in the shape of an avian skull. Scanner lenses glitter in the sockets of its eyes. Clusters of antennae and sensors halo its head. Its hands are tipped in silvered blades. This is the Observer of the Court of Assassins, and she is called Noor.

The second newcomer is tall, perhaps even as tall as Hekkarron. Robes of light-eating fabric swath its shape so that it appears to have no dimension. A human skull grins from beneath its cowl. She is called Theta and by ancient agreement she comes from the temple of the Culexus. She is soulless, one of those cursed by the Pariah gene to be a blank absence in the sea of souls. The craft of her temple has taken that quality and moulded it so that she is a vortex of despair and oblivion walking in flesh. She is the Voice of the Abyss, though she speaks rarely, and what she says means death or life.

Cradus limps to stand beside the Observer and the Voice so that they form a grim triumvirate facing Ancia and Hekkarron across the circular abyss.

'These are my... fellows of the Court,' says Cradus, 'the Voice of the Abyss, and the Observer of the Court. I am sure–'

'I know who they are, Cradus,' says Hekkarron. 'There is no need to gild this grotesquery further.'

'Come, come, where are the fine manners you showed outside?' Cradus shows his corpse-like smile. 'I had always found the Custodians to have a fine sense of formality and decorum.'

Cradus glances at the still figure of the Voice, and then back to Hekkarron, smiling. 'Or is it that something is grating on your nerves?'

'We come to take a weapon that was passed into your keeping,' says Hekkarron, ignoring the Keeper's jibe.

'Is that so?' asks Cradus. 'Many weapons have been given to us over the years by your order. Some so that we can understand their nature. Some to use. Some to bury out of sight or memory.' He pauses, the grin widening beneath his mask. 'But all of them are ours to keep.'

'A sword was sent to you this night,' says Hekkarron. 'It must have been here no more than five hours, and you shall return it to me, now.'

'And I thought that diplomacy was part of your training.' Cradus shakes his head in a pantomime display of disappointment.

'Have you seen the world outside?' asks Ancia. 'The Palace itself burns, and creatures of the warp dance in the blaze.'

Cradus shrugs. 'You think that this is the first calamity that has befallen the Throneworld? It is not the first, nor is it the first occasion that those who would protect it come to our doors demanding that we yield the secrets we keep. One hour in our keeping or ten thousand years, it makes no difference. The sword remains with us.'

'You are risking everything, you understand?' Ancia's face is a picture of disbelief. 'Everything.'

'We understand,' says Cradus, and the mock humour is gone from his tone now. 'More than you we understand what one weapon, one moment, one person in the right place and time, can do. That is why we must deny you what you ask.'

There is silence. Then Hekkarron nods.

'Very well,' he says, and half turns. The gesture is supremely human, casual, relaxed and resigned. He looks away from the three Assassins, and steps towards the door. 'Come, Ancia.'

She does not move.

'No, Warden.' Her voice is brittle ice. 'We haven't been given what we came for.'

'You heard the Honoured Keeper – the Officio have a duty to keep what is given to them even from us.'

'I heard, and for all that I think that the Honoured Keeper defecates when he speaks, I understand the bindings of duty.' She smiles now. It's her turn. 'Which is why they are going to give you the sword.'

Cradus shakes his head as though at a weak joke. 'You could kill everyone in this tower and tear it down stone by stone, and you would never have the weapon you seek.'

'I did not say we would take it,' says Ancia. 'I said you were going to give it to the Warden.'

'Ludicrous…' says Cradus.

Ancia is still smiling.

'Forgive me, my memory for matters of duty and tradition is not as sharp as Warden Hekkarron's, but from recollection, the Officio Assassinorum is bound to honour the execution orders it receives, is it not?'

'You are correct,' says Cradus, 'but that does not–'

'You have a kill order issued many millennia ago and reissued several times by inquisitors and lords militant, and Solar Commanders. That order is for the slaying of a single renegade Space Marine of unknown origin – a renegade designated as Cypher. So far, you have failed to eliminate the target despite – oh, let me see – the passing of several thousand years, thirty-four attempts, and the loss of four of your operatives. Excuse me if I am a little vague on some of the details.'

'What of it?' asks Cradus.

'He is here,' replies Ancia. 'That target is here.'

'On Terra?'

'In the Palace itself.' Ancia nods at the figure with the avian skull mask. 'The Observer of the Court of Assassins should surely know this… unless the title is largely honorary.'

'Your tone is not acceptable, augur,' snaps Cradus.

Ancia bows her head briefly. 'Forgive me, something must be grating on my nerves.' She glances at the Voice of the Abyss and then back at Cradus. 'The target you have failed to bring down for thousands of years is here, now, and he is seeking the sword. Give it to us and it will draw him out, and you can be there to fulfil the duty of your Officio. All you will need to do is comply.'

'How certain are you of what you say?'

'We all have our uses, Keeper. Mine is knowing something of the future. Tell me again, what's yours?'

Hekkarron raises a hand, cutting through the exchange.

'I am willing to extend the offer suggested by Augur Ancia to the Officio on behalf of the Adeptus Custodes,' he says. 'Do you agree to it?'

There is quiet for a moment. Ancia and Hekkarron watch the Assassins. They played a good game, don't you think?

When the quiet breaks it is not Cradus that speaks but Theta, the Voice of the Abyss.

'We agree, Custodian,' she says. 'The sword shall be brought forth.'

'You have the thanks of the Throne,' says Hekkarron, and he gives a nod that is as close to a bow as a Custodian will give anyone other than the Emperor.

'Do not thank us,' says the Voice of the Abyss. 'Some gifts have a price, Custodian. Even those blind to the future know that…'

With that the three of them withdraw like a mist driven by the wind.

TEN

Azkhar's Mindscape

Rain is falling in the forest, heavy drops that send the canopy shivering and fill the air with whispers. Azkhar opens what he thinks are his eyes. The trunks and branches of trees rise about him, scraping a grey sky with dark leaves and twisted branches. He stands and takes a step. He can see a clear patch of light about. Rain strikes his face. He raises his head so that the droplets run down his cheeks, and onto his lips and tongue. He knows the taste of this rain. It tastes of home.

'So, this is what it looked like,' says a voice.

Azkhar turns. A man is sitting on a cairn of moss-covered stone. He wears a robe of off-white, and the hood covering his head half hides a face the colour of copper. Azkhar looks at the man for a long moment, and then turns his gaze around the circle of twisted trees. It is all so familiar, so real, and utterly impossible.

'Yes,' says Azkhar. His voice is calm. The anger that edged it before gone. Now he sounds like a soul that has realised it has reached the end of a journey. 'This is Caliban, just as it was… before the Lion, before Luther, before the Imperium. Before us.' Azkhar glances at the hooded figure. 'But, of course, you will never have seen it before.'

'You know who I am?' asks the hooded figure.

'Of course. You were on the bridge in the Imperial Palace. You are a Librarian of the Dark Angels Chapter that bears the name and shame of the Legion I once belonged to.'

'You belong to it still,' says Mordachi, 'as do I.'

Azkhar laughs. His face is younger here, cleaner, his features without the sneer that creases his expression in the real world.

'You really believe that, don't you? But you know it's a lie. The Legion is long dead. I am just a relic of its mistakes and you an echo of its pride.'

'That is not true,' says Mordachi. He stands and lowers his hood. The bonded studs and tattoos of rank and initiation mark his skin. 'You are my brother, and though you have strayed and fallen, you can repent. Redemption can be yours.'

'Mine? Or yours, Librarian?' Azkhar gestures at the forest surrounding them. 'We are standing in my thoughts and memories, but in reality we are somewhere inside the Imperial Palace on Terra. What deeds have you done to come here, Librarian? What new sins have you piled on the old ones just so that you can offer me redemption?'

'My conscience is clear.'

'As is mine.'

The two look at each other for a long moment. The trees whisper and the rain falls in this place that is a dream of a world long gone.

'You betrayed the Lion,' says Mordachi at last. 'You turned

on your brothers. You gave your loyalty to things of darkness. Do you feel no shame for that?'

'No,' says Azkhar. 'No, I do not. They were all fools and liars. For you to betray someone they must be worthy of loyalty.'

Mordachi does not respond to that, but looks away, at the green leaves and falling rain.

'This is not the normal way of things, is it? You do not normally bring us into dreamscapes of the past and offer us redemption while the rain falls, do you?'

'There are many things you do not know or understand, traitor.'

Azkhar shakes his head. There is no bitterness in the expression; if anything there is understanding.

'I have heard of your interrogations from some of your brothers that we once captured. They told us much, though they did not want to. Your skull-faced Chaplains are the ones to offer redemption and give question. Your kind are the aides, and diviners of truth, not redeemers.'

'Cruelty is not the only way to forgiveness,' says Mordachi. 'Just the path that most decide to take.'

'Is that so? What are those other paths?'

'Confession, penance.' The mind image of Mordachi shifts and the trees shake. A peal of thunder sounds. Azkhar glances around, and there is a smile on his face.

'Is time running short, Librarian? You are as much a fugitive in the Palace as we are. All this time you are spending in my mind, you risk discovery, and there is the fact of *what* you are and *where* you are...'

The rain has stopped. The wind picks up. The trees begin to shed their leaves. The ground is shaking. The image of Mordachi looks around. His skin is cracking. There are voices on the wind, calling.

'You are a witch, Librarian. Being here, on Terra, close to the Golden Throne is a burden I am glad I don't have to bear.'

Mordachi can hear the voices clearly now. He is trying to shut them out. His will is strong, very strong. You don't become an Epistolary in the Librarius of the Dark Angels without a will that could break iron. But the psychic pressure is building and even the strongest man cannot hold back an ocean.

'You are not here to redeem me, are you? You do not have time to persuade me of my sins. No, you are here because you need something from me.'

Mordachi stills the tremor in his thoughts and the forest and wind calm. The image of his face becomes whole again. Azkhar is watching him, still smiling the boyish smile that has not been his to wear for millennia.

'It's him, isn't it – Cypher? You want him. I don't blame you, I hunted him too, once. I failed. You see, your kind might hate us, or pity us, or want to redeem us. But me, I loathe him and always have.'

In reply Mordachi nods. The gesture and the words are an effort that sends a fork of lightning across the sky.

'Where is the one called Cypher going? What will he do next?'

Mordachi is trying to hold onto the telepathic link with Azkhar, but the warp is churning and the voices on the wind are razor shrieks.

'You are going to kill me, Dark Angel,' says Azkhar. 'Redemption or no, that is certain. But I think I have one betrayal left in me.'

The forest is gone now. Azkhar and Mordachi's dream images stand on a grey infinity. Azkhar's smile broadens.

'Do you want to know a secret?'

* * *

The Court Of Assassins

Cradus sits in a room of stone. It is set high in the side of the tower that houses the Court of Assassins. Grey snowflakes gather in the corners. The bones and feathers of dead crows skitter and tumble across the floor. The room has no door. Its single window is a ragged hole, a wound left by a missile that struck long ago. There is no furniture. It is just a space enclosed by walls. Cradus sits on the floor, back bent, atop a closed metal aperture. The robes of his office as Keeper of the Court hang from him. A mask still covers his eyes. He shifts. His bones ache. The age of his appearance lies heavy on him.

You see, to an Assassin of the Callidus Temple, the face they wear holds an element of truth. When they become a beggar child, or warlord, they take on that person's life. The pains, the language, the preoccupations, all of it. They pull on that heavy skin of another life and for a while they live with them, two people intertwined in one body. They think as both Assassin and person; they live as them, if only for the time they wear their face. How else can they pass undetected? Anything else would be a compromise to their craft, and the Officio Assassinorum do not compromise.

'Must I do this deed?' asks Cradus aloud. His voice is weary, but that and the words are ritualised. Everything about Cradus' existence is a ritual without a god.

They are called Assassin *temple*s, remember, and the name is not an affectation. They are ancient entities, old when the Emperor unified Terra. Callidus, Venenum, Vindicare, Culexus, Vanus, Eversor: they are not just divisions of the methodology in murder; they are creeds in adoration. Their adepts do not simply exist to kill, but to kill in a particular way, conforming to an art in preparation and execution.

Silence answers Cradus' question. He is aware of the time that has passed, and the lives that he has lived. He can remember the child that was taken from their home as it burned. He can remember the training, the lethal games of deception and speed. He can see the first face he took. An old woman who sold candles to pilgrims next to a cathedral, here on Terra. He can still hear her voice, a ghost on his lips, calling out to those that pass.

'Light! Light to carry your prayer to the Emperor! Light!' She would brandish the candles at those that passed. Some would stop, and drop a coin into the iron box that hung from her back, and take a candle. She worried about the pain in her fingers, and what had become of her daughter who had gone to the Southern Zones five years before and never come back. She had watched the pilgrims until the one that had been marked came.

He looked much like the rest. The roughness of his robes and sandals covered the fact that he had both money and power in excess. They, just like this pilgrimage, were a sham, a penance paid for his crimes. Those crimes had many shades. There were the cruelties and atrocities that he committed, but they would not have been enough to condemn him to death at the hand of the Officio. No, the crimes that wrote and sealed his death warrant were that he had used his position to skim resources and people from the Emperor's tithe, that he was edging towards governorship of a planet, a sector even; that he dreamed of breaking with the Imperium and making his own empire. But his subtlety did not equal his ambition. So, he died. He died crushed by a block of stone displaced by micro-charges from the cathedral edifice as he bent to take a candle from Cradus' hand.

Cradus closes his eyes behind his mask at the memory. Two

decades later, the man's son had come to the same spot. The son was not the father, but he had taken on his father's crimes and ambitions. He was more dangerous than the father, more subtle, more careful. He had come to light a candle for his father's soul at the place he died. Once he had done that, the son had a path of fire that he would walk. Cradus was there to hand the son the candle and watch as he bent to light it, and to see his skull crushed. There are many ways that the son could have died, ways sharp and bloody, but he met his end as his father had, on that spot, struck by a shard sliced from the same broken stone. That is what murder as art means. It means ritual. It means that every detail matters.

In the cold cell in the stone tower, Cradus takes the mask from his face. Light touches the eyes beneath. He is not blind now. He can see the objects that lie on the floor in front of him. The first is a splinter of black ceramite. It was sliced from my armour by the last Assassin that I met. The Officio retrieved it along with the body. It is a kill token, a physical representation of the death-debt that the Assassins owe me. Alongside it, on a bed of red velvet, lies an injector and a crystal vial of liquid. Cradus looks at them. His mind is still, the memories of old faces fading. His thoughts are empty, a tablet of wax scraped clean before the stylus cuts into it.

He touches the shard of armour, then picks up the injector, loads the vial into it and puts it to his neck. He bids goodbye to the Keeper that he has been. He squeezes the trigger.

He feels nothing at first. He puts the injector down. In his mind he holds an image of a new self. The metal seal beneath him begins to descend into the floor. The aperture closes above him. Darkness surrounds him. The metal seal is now a platform sliding down a shaft. The walls are smooth. He feels the drug unfold into his blood. Cradus' consciousness explodes.

Memories, images, ideas and thoughts tumble in a black void. His cells writhe. Cradus holds a single strand of thought: the idea of a self. If his grip on this strand slips, his body will dissolve. Bones will become slime. Flesh will become liquid. The explosion of his thoughts will boil off into a last scream of madness before he dies. He holds to the strand and the darkness slides past.

Polymorphine... the sacred drug of the Callidus. Inject it into a normal human and they will die in agony as their body and mind tear themselves apart. Flesh becomes plastic to the mind, down to the cellular level. For almost every sentient creature that means death. The mind is not meant to control its host. Thoughts are fickle. Flesh demands constancy. So to link the two is death. Not to the Callidus. The polymorphine allows them to change themselves. They can become anyone. They can slip the life and appearance on like a new skin. With implants laced into their bones and muscles they can even assume shapes a long way from human. It takes years of training for an Assassin to master the shape-shifter drug. For every one that succeeds, many do not, and to fail is to die.

Impressive, of course, but how did the founders of the temple survive for long enough to both discover the power of the drug and perfect their mastery of it? Think about it. Polymorphine is completely lethal. Moreover, the way it kills is from beyond nightmare. So what of the first who took it? What of the second, and third, and the rest? They saw what happened to those that came before and persisted. What about the first to survive? Is there an antecedent of all Callidus? A single being wracked by agony, their shape changing and changing again? A horror and abomination that somehow survived and taught others? Perhaps. I would like to know, but if they know the truth the Callidus do not tell.

Cradus sheds the shape of the Keeper. That body was old. The one that replaces it is not. Muscles fill. Bones thicken. Skin smooths. Scars spread over his back and across his body. Burns as white splashes. Knots of tissue where bullet wounds have healed. The criss-cross of blade cuts. They are Cradus' memory of every injury he has suffered in his service to the temple. The form he has assumed is not someone else's face, it is his own. Or at least his image of himself.

He reaches the bottom of the shaft. Cold light replaces the black. The descent stops. Cradus rises, shedding the Keeper's cloak. His back is no longer bent. Muscles flow under their shroud of scars. He looks no older than thirty, but his eyes are ancient.

The chamber is small, spherical. The glow-globes that float in the air are cracked. Strings of bird and lizard skulls hang from the roof. There are cylinders scattered on the floor. They glitter with energy fields. Heavy rusted locks snap free of their lids as he places his hand on them. Liquid fills the space inside, dark and viscous. He pulls out the tools and devices from the fluid. The bio-inert liquid pools on the floor under each of the wicked things: the phase sword, the knives, the needle implants, neural shredder, digi-weapons, grav-chute, blind grenades and all the rest. He does this without ceremony, sometimes tossing the things down to ooze on the stone. Everything is ritual, and everything matters, but these are just tools. Cradus is the weapon.

He slides a few of the objects into slits in his skin and into hidden cavities in his bones. It's fast, almost a dance, the movements repeated so many times through his life that they are like breathing. He sprays black synskin over his flesh. He leaves his face bare. He wipes equipment dry, sheathes weapons. Last, he picks up the ragged Keeper's cloak and settles it over his shoulders. Without the setting of the Court, it is just a dirty fall of fabric.

'Must I do this deed?' he asks again. He has the sliver of ceramite from my armour in his hand.

He must ask the question, you see. That is part of the paradox of an organisation that lives for death. It must be reluctant. If it was not, well… that's how we end up here, with the stars bleeding crimson.

'It is willed. It is written, and it must be,' he answers himself. He pulls the hood over his head, then takes the shard of my armour and tucks it into his sash. The ritual is done. He is remade. He is shriven, and he is coming to kill me.

I wonder if he will succeed.

ELEVEN

Northern Zone Communication Hub

Everyone expects someone who is hunted to run. That is the story we all know – the fugitive lucky enough to get free runs across the land, the hounds at their heels, panic in their breath, fear in their eyes as they look behind. That is the way most hunts play out. And the end, well, we know that, too, don't we? The prey brought down, torn apart, left as bloody tatters on the ground. We know that part of the story; we expect it, and know that's always how it goes. That is why we like the idea of the other story, the one that never happens – the fugitive who through guile and strength and persistence not only eludes their hunters, but finds forgiveness for their crimes. As a species we like that story. We like its impossible promise of hope.

Is this that type of story? I think it unlikely, don't you?

Apart from anything else, I am not running. I am going into the teeth of the hounds. And I am not without teeth of my own.

A streak of plasma burns across the cavern space, and hits a fuel transit node. A ball of red-orange flame punches into the air, folding over itself as it washes across the vaulted roof. Beneath its glow the communication knave gleams with blood and metal. Screams and smoke boil through the air.

This is the main communication hub for this level of the Palace. Messages pass through here in an endless flow of runners, scroll tubes, data-conduits and code crystals. Banks of desks and equipment sit in deep rows. A menagerie of creatures and humans dwell here, feeding off the circulation of data. Messengers trained in coded memory techniques wait in pens, their feet replaced by sprung augmetics, their mouths sipping nutrient paste from tubes so that they can run the hundreds of miles from one part of the Palace to another. Cyber-ibis wait in cages to fly free with data-capsules slotted into their skulls. Even with the Palace locked down and on a war footing, it is a place of constant activity. At least seven hundred souls are present beneath its roof at any time.

We hit it without warning and without mercy. A rolling wall of explosions and gunfire announces our presence. A wall in the main section of the vaulted chamber blows in. We come out of the breach and begin killing. Eight of us. Only eight. There are hundreds in the chamber. It will not take us long to make it none.

A platoon of Solar Hoplites guard the chamber's doors: fifty soldiers in gilded copper, with high-crested helmets and wide-barrelled blast-lasers. Not a small force, but we are legionaries, and we have been exercising the craft of war for as long as this Palace has stood. Fifty against eight, five hundred against eight, five thousand against eight: it does not matter. They do not stand a chance.

We are here for two reasons. The first is tactical. This is a main node of communication in this part of the Palace. We destroy it, and we are cloaked by the inability of the defenders to hear and deduce what is happening. It is not a good reason, is it? In truth, it is not going to be particularly effective either. The Palace is already burning, and what can we do that the power of the false gods cannot do better?

No, the real reason is that someone will notice what we have done. Hekkarron, my brief gaoler, will be coming after me. It is not in the nature of a Custodian to relent or to relinquish a duty. He will be searching, and with him will be the sword. Where else could it have gone? Perhaps Hekkarron or one of his kin even recognised the nature of the blade I carried. He will have it. If he is hunting me, he will notice if something like this communication hub is destroyed. He will notice, and he will start to think and to deduce that it is me who has lit this fire and he will be drawn to it. That is all I need this massacre to achieve, and what we have to do now is make sure the fires we light burn bright enough.

I walk through the unfolding carnage and the pistols in my hands sing their song. A panicked wave of message scriveners scrambles past the soldiers, faces wide with terror. A squad of hoplites runs down a near corridor between shelves of scroll tubes, firing as they move. Their shots cook the air and kiss my armour. Brave. Very brave. I fire, and the stream of plasma dances from the muzzle of my gun. I take the last soldier in the line with a shot to the head that burns through his skull and strikes the man behind him. My bolt pistol speaks an instant later. The bolt shell hits another hoplite as their head twitches to see what has happened. The mass-reactive component in this shell is keyed to explode only after two impacts. The bolt shell passes through their skull in a spray of red and hits the gun casing of the soldier behind them. Gun and shell explode. A cloud of copper shrapnel and white heat cuts into the fleeing crowd nearby. Several souls reaped with one cut of the scythe, and I am still firing and taking from the living with each squeeze of the trigger.

What? Did you expect me to be merciful? Did you expect me to be kind? I am neither. No one is innocent in this universe. No one...

'Thy souls to reap!' rasps Bakhariel, close to me. 'Thy souls to keep!'

He is moving like an image jammed in a pict-feed. Yellow-and-green light is sweating off him. I see him raise his hand and the gesture dissolves a block of shelves and people into ash. His voice is coming from his mind as much as his mouth, shaking frost and blood from the air. His shadow is a bloated cloak dragged behind him. Eyes and claws flicker in the gloom.

'The eye opens!' shouts Bakhariel. 'Crimson is the path!' He shudders and the circle of reality around him vanishes into pink flame and burning blood.

Korlael turns from his own slaughter to look at Bakhariel. Can he see what I know? Does he sense what is coming, too? He takes a step towards Bakhariel, perhaps to restrain him, and in that moment Korlael does not see the enemy come for him.

'For Terra!'

The war cry vibrates through the smoke-laced air. The warrior comes out of the flames. He is a blur of yellow ceramite. Lightning sheathes his left fist. The symbol of a clenched obsidian gauntlet sits on his left arm. He is one of the Imperial Fists, the descendants of those that once stood on the walls of Terra, and who still stand as praetorians of the Throneworld. I have not seen one of their breed in a thousand years. I had not thought to see one now. They should have been on the walls where the greater battle rages… Should have been, but chance does not care what should have been.

The Imperial Fist comes right at Korlael, firing. Explosions burst on my brother's armour. Chunks of ceramite and metal tear free. Korlael does not fall, but staggers, and that is all the opening the Imperial Fist needs. This one is a veteran. He knows the craft of war as only one who has given his body and blood to it can.

Korlael brings his sword up in time to meet the charge, and then the two are a blur of lightning and steel. Chips of plasteel and ceramite scatter from the kiss of blade and shield. The Imperial Fist takes the blows, and then rams his fist forwards.

Sword and fist meet. Lightning splits the air and thunder splits the cacophony of battle. The yellow-armoured warrior is coming forward, ramming the shield edge into Korlael's helm. Eye-lenses shatter. Korlael's blade is already spinning in his grip, rising only to fall like a thunderbolt, and the Imperial Fist's shield is bracing to meet the blow.

This is the tableau held in my eye as I turn my head to see it. Here I am seeing the Imperium's glory and folly held still, in the instant between falling sword and rising shield meeting. Two warriors, one old in battle, the other seeming younger but who has lived countless lifetimes. The fire of ruin is rising behind them. I can see Korlael's eyes in the shattered lenses of his helm. I can see the old warrior of the Imperial Fists brace to take the sword blow on his shield.

This is a fight that will never end. Here or amongst the stars or in the infinity of time it will play out between lone warriors or between countless armies. It is fated.

But I have never liked fate, and my patience has its limits.

Three shots. One to smash the Imperial Fist off his feet. The second to rip open the join of his armour around the throat. Then the blast of plasma to the chest to burn through his valiant hearts. As I say, my patience has its limits. For a moment, as I watch the corpse of this fine warrior fall to the ground, and hear the screams of the innocent, it feels right. It feels good to be a killer and an agent of misrule.

Please tell me you are not surprised.

TWELVE

Azkhar's Mindscape

'Do you wish absolution?' asks Mordachi.

It is quiet in the space of Azkhar's dying mind. Mordachi's question hangs for a second as he looks down at my brother. Azkhar is fading, the image of his face unravels into smoke. He has just betrayed me. Treachery, it seems, is a habit as much as a choice.

'Absolution?' says Azkhar, and chuckles. 'How do you imagine I could come by that, Dark Angel? The secrets I have told you only push me further beyond the reach of any forgiveness.'

'Confess,' says Mordachi. 'Ask for forgiveness. Accept your fate.' He is earnest. At this moment he would give almost anything for Azkhar to agree.

'So simple?'

'Yes.'

'If only that were true.' The space around Azkhar is open, blank, a sheet of paper waiting for a pen. The scream of the psychic wind has stopped. This is a moment suspended in a length of time no longer than a heartbeat – a tick unfolding to the tock.

Mordachi does not know why he has not ended this encounter. He has what he needs and more. He knows he should not linger. The quiet is an illusion of calm.

'You are killing me now, aren't you, Dark Angel?' asks Azkhar. 'The sand of my time is done.'

'Yes.'

Azkhar nods to himself. 'At last. None of us deserve to survive, you know, and none of us shall. There is hope in that, at least. I hope you catch *him*. He deserves the kind of forgiveness you offer.'

Azkhar turns his head and as he does the ghost of the forests of Caliban opens in front of him again. The rain is falling on his face.

'It was better then. All that time ago – it was better then.'

Mordachi holds his thoughts still for an instant more. Somewhere inside him, something in his soul has changed. He knows it but does not know how.

'Is there more that you wish to say?' asks Mordachi.

Azkhar smiles one last time.

'More than you will ever know.'

Then the image of the young warrior in robes and the forests of Caliban is gone. Mordachi is alone in the white void for a moment more, and then he opens his eyes in the physical world.

Northern Zone

The wind blowing through the sewage tunnel is hot and holds no smell of forest or rain. Mordachi takes his hand from where it rests on Azkhar's skull. Frost has burned both his fingers and the flesh of Azkhar's face. My brother's eyes are open, staring at nothing. Mordachi looks at him for a second, feeling the psychic backwash shiver through his muscles like a fever. Behind him Nariel waits.

'Did he give us anything?' asks Nariel.

'He gave us everything.' Mordachi stands. Around him the desolate tangle of the Imperial Palace sings with the sound of ghost winds. Somewhere, far off, he can hear gunfire.

'Burn the body and the armour,' says Mordachi. 'No trace.'

'Did he tell you what Cypher–'

'Cypher is going to the Sanctum Imperialis, brother. He means to reach the Throne Room.'

Which is more important, the truth or what people believe? Most would say the truth, but that is too easy. No one actually *wants* the truth. Not in this universe. Hearing the truth is like looking on the face of a god – you have a moment of pure revelation, and then you are ash carried away to oblivion, knowing nothing, seeing nothing. When people say they want the truth, they mean that they want something they can understand, something that fits, that they can carry around in their thoughts like a relic, to touch and take away the fear of what they are living.

Am I a traitor? Am I one soul, or am I many? Have I had many names or only the one? Do I wish redemption or vengeance? It's comforting to be able to pick one, and then see everything fall into line behind it – villain-hero, right-wrong, on and on. That's what people want when they ask for the truth. They want the lie that makes the world simple.

But you are not like that, are you? You know that it is better not to ask for the truth. That what you should ask for are secrets.

* * *

Lion's Gate

'You think the Assassins will keep their word?' asks Ancia.

'I do. They will deliver the sword as agreed.'

'But they did not let us walk away with it in our hands.'

'I doubt it was there. They have other places where they keep their instruments of murder. The sword will come to us, but not before the trap is set.'

'They are following us, though. There are shadows and guns on us even now.'

'Of course. What else did you expect of them?'

Listen now. Not to what the Custodian Warden and the Doomscryer are saying. Listen to their fears and realisation materialise. It's coming. It's close now. Listen and you will learn something…

Hekkarron and Ancia are in the Lion's Gate central transit cavern when the communication comes through. A signal buzz inside Hekkarron's helm. It's chopped with static, but Hekkarron understands it. The Custodian vox-network, unlike much of the infrastructure in the Palace, is still functioning. Barely. He raises a hand to halt the conversation with Ancia for the seconds it takes him to digest the signal and issue a reply.

'There was an attack on the Northern Zone Communication Hub,' he says, lowering his hand. 'No survivors.'

The transit cavern is almost deserted. The hoist carriages and macro-rail haulers that cross through it have been halted. The crowds of loaders and guards and officials are absent. Only a few with fear writ plain in their eyes hover at the edge of platforms and gates. Wind blows through the open transit passages. Ancia and Hekkarron have paused here on their journey back from the Court of Assassins. A Custodian grav-tank summoned by Hekkarron is already inbound to their location. Ancia closes her eyes as she absorbs the news. In her mind she is threading memory and oracular vision.

'It was him,' she says. 'It was Cypher.'

'He is trying to find the location of the sword,' says Hekkarron. He is genuinely confused. 'That kind of mayhem does not serve that aim…'

And now, here comes a revelation.

'Unless…' Ancia's eyes are flicking across the empty platform in front of her. She is seeing her thoughts and possible futures and what she is beginning to glimpse is terrifying. 'Unless we are wrong. Unless the sword isn't what he is after now.'

'What do you mean?'

'The images he was thinking of in the cell…'

'The sword?'

'Yes… It filled his mind.'

She is swaying now, eyes closed. The air is crackling around her. In her skull she is not just seeing the psychoactive image she pulled from my cell – she is reliving it, drawing the warp into the memory so that it is more than an image, so that it is a connection to the past. She sees me sitting in my cell. She sees the sword as I saw it with my thoughts, clear and true.

'You could taste the thought of the sword on the stone he touched. That thought was everything… But…' She winces. She is very close now to realising something that I haven't told you. 'But what if it was a lie?'

In her mind she turns her gaze from the sword to the ghost image of my face as I sat in my cell. And she sees that I was looking at her from the past, and that I was smiling.

'He knew we would come,' she breathes. 'Somehow he knew. He left the thought and image of the sword there for us to find. He is not coming for the sword. We have made a mistake. He is going somewhere else.'

And there it is.

Did you see that coming before we arrived here?

Do you feel aggrieved that I have not been telling you the truth? You shouldn't; after all, you should know better than to ask for something that you cannot have.

'Where is he going?' asks Hekkarron.

The air is spinning around Ancia now as she stands on the deserted platform. Static crackles. Paint is peeling off the struts and pillars holding the roof above her. At the other end of the platform a high official looks at her and begins to scream. Her mind is going to other places now, into future paths and images of what might be. They do not call them Doomscryers for nothing. The rest of her abilities are fine tricks, but this is what she exists for – to know what will happen before it does.

'He is going to...'

And she begins to see it then – the light, the sword, and the figure wrapped in gold and cables, and another figure kneeling, a sword in its hand, a broken sword, a sword that will never break, eyes opening in a face that is a skull, eyes shut in a face like stone that has not moved in ten thousand years, on and on, image drawn over image in ghost light and the colour of dreams. She sees...

'The future is breaking and repeating.'

'Where is Cypher going?' Hekkarron asks, but he knows; deep in the fear he does not have, he knows. 'Speak what you see.'

'This should not be happening. The future is converging but changing between the same two paths second by second. There should be many paths... There should...'

'Ancia, speak.'

She does not want to. She can face horrors that would break any human, but at this moment she is seeing everything narrow to a single point, a single choice that will cleave time in two. But she can also see the answer to Hekkarron's question, because it is the place where this story has to lead.

'The Throne Room,' she answers. 'The Emperor, he means to reach the Emperor.'

'He cannot believe that he could do it...' says Hekkarron.

'He does,' she replies as insight floods her. 'Light of the Throne, it is why he came to Terra. We chained him next to where he wanted to reach all along. He knows a way into the Inner Sanctum... He has a way in. A way you have missed...'

'Where?'

'I am... I cannot see clearly...'

'You must!'

'The Path of Martyrs... Something there, something will happen there... but it is not clear...'

But she does not finish the sentence because Hekkarron is already running, and a golden grav-tank is spearing down out of the night.

'Return to the Dark Cells, augur,' he calls as he leaps from the edge of the platform onto the tank. Ancia is still quivering, the force of her vision spidering the air with static. She hears his command, and almost calls after him that there is something else, something on the edge of her sight that he should know, but then the vision fades, and the grav-tank is speeding into the distance.

The Imperial Palace

There is a world beneath the skin of existence. I am sure you have heard that before, an easy metaphor for lies or greater truths, or for things that are both. In the Imperial Palace it is not just a metaphor – it is a literal reality. It is not just a complex of buildings, it is a scab healed over history. The history of the Imperium, of humanity, all of it is here, crushed underneath the weight of the past.

Let me show you.

We start high in the night sky. Beneath us lies Terra. Lights dot the curve of its face. They are the lights of hab-districts the size of ancient empires, of pilgrim camps that have ossified into rockcrete, of administrative palaces that consume billions of tons of parchment and ink in a single day. Beside those lights are fires, great blazes that snake across the land. Great smudges of smoke blur their glow. People are dying in that light. Hundreds of thousands of souls cooking to ash, screaming, pleading with their last breaths.

Millions die every day on this world. They die from hunger in hive blocks. They die to the knives of gangs. They die to the diseases that pollution has seeded into their bones. No one marks them, and the world does not shake on its axis because of their passing. There are too many reasons for them dying, too many tragedies, to make the universe treat them with anything but callous indifference. Those being slaughtered in the fires and battles tonight... those deaths are not going unnoticed. The warp is singing with pain and rage and despair. People far beyond the Palace are clutching prayer scripts and waking from sleep with shivers of dread. The world is shaking and all the souls clinging to its skin can feel it.

Why? Why does this slaughter and conflagration make existence sit up and take notice when the deaths of just as many pass unmarked every day? Because they are not dying and suffering for many reasons but because of one cause, because a war has taken them, and that war might be the beginning of the end of everything.

Our view is moving now, dragged in by the sight of the

Imperial Palace. It has a field of gravity in the mind. It pulls our minds inexorably towards it. It is a continent, larger than the kingdoms and empires that ancient warlords carved over the face of the world. Once we are below the atmosphere its scattered lights are their own cosmos, pulled from the heavens and laid across the ground. It is truly vast. You wonder how we and Mordachi's Dark Angels can hunt and hide in the sacred heart of the Imperium? How can we hide and fight and go unnoticed? It is because the Palace is not a building or a city. There are districts of warehouses here. Spaces piled with stores of parchment and food that have long rotted, and great forests of fungi. Shrine complexes to saints that no one remembers that have not heard the tread of a human foot in centuries. Hab-blocks crammed with candle lighters, inscribers and refuse gleaners. All of those can be found in one small part of the Palace. Its lights, seen from the sky above, are its most flattering face. As our view comes level with the highest towers, we begin to see the rot under the gleam.

From above the towers and domes that ring the Inner Sanctum, you plunge down. The stone and bronze spires reach up to greet you like knives. You see it all: the Ten Towers of the Dawn, the Black Ministry, the Bastion Magna; your eyes are filled with the light of the fires burning at the edge of sight. You can smell the smoke on the wind. You are almost at the height of the tallest towers now. You can see the grime-covered glass in their windows, and glimpse the expressions of grotesques and gargoyles as they flash past.

You see the crows that have made these ancient stones their parliaments; you see, through rotten holes in roofs, great rooms, which are now only gathering places for the excrement of carrion; you see the corpse and skull-grin of a man who climbed up to see the sun a century ago, dried and picked clean. You see all this and know that this is only the most recent layer of the city that is a palace.

On you dive, and now you might well be falling. The canyons between buildings open, and down you go. You fall past balconies, and bridges, and tangles of cable strung across the gulfs as though to bind the vast structures together.

You see people now, hundreds of them, maybe thousands of them, rushing along roads and bridges. A building is burning. It is the size of a mountain. The fire is blazing from its core as thousands of years of parchment records burn. Orange tongues spill from its windows, and the population that called it home flee. You can see an old man stumble and grip the child in his arms. High above, the spire of the building begins to creak as the fire scoops out its heart. Pieces of masonry begin to fall. The old man begins to hurry with the surge of the crowd flowing across the bridge. He and the child might survive, or might not. There is nothing you can do. You are only here to watch.

And now you are past them, and so far down in the dark that the sky is just a jagged slit above. And then it is gone and there is only darkness. A brief moment of perfect darkness as you pass through the roof of the Avenue of Ascension and see the statues looking down at the last few robed figures hurrying, ringed by soldiers, fear in all their eyes. They glitter with rings and chains that could buy starships or ransom planets. They have lived all their lives in here, in the world of stone and dust and lost memory that is this palace. And now they can smell the smoke and feel the heat of the fire of change. And they are afraid.

You pass them, and move down through the layers of rockcrete and marble, through the layers of mausoleums and ossuaries. You dive through the lakes of poison that have gathered in caverns. You go on and on, down and down through history crushed by the ages that followed it. There are cities down here beneath the world, cities, and temples and streets drowned in lightless water. There are people and the beasts that hunt them, there are the corpses of god machines, there are paths and there are doors. There are secrets that no one knows, because down here at the root of the world nothing is lost, only forgotten…

THIRTEEN

Catacombs

Down in the black root of the world is where you find me and my eight remaining brothers. All that you have seen is context for what will happen now. We fled the ambush by Mordachi, down into the depths. We are moving along a buried road between half-collapsed stone pillars. The road is paved with white marble, now cracked and filmed with algae. Carvings wind around the pillars showing the deeds of kings and queens long dead. The roof above is a curve of debris held together by luck.

We are not the only ones who have come to shelter from the present in the underworld. People have fled down here from portions of the Palace that are burning. Whether some of them knew of the paths below, or if they just followed the old, human instinct to flee into the deep places, I do not know.

There are crowds cowering at the edges of the old pillared road, families of scribes, parents clutching infants, old and young, wealthy and poor, hunched around the light of oil fires.

They begin to scream and flee when they see us: giants in black armour with red eyes. Some brave soul with a gun shoots at us. We ignore it. We have no reason to do anything else. Then Bakhariel begins to slow, and then he stops.

'Come closer...' he burbles. 'The night, the burning moon, the grinding wound... They come closer.'

Korlael slows and turns to hurry his brother on.

'Brother, we need to keep moving.'

'No... no... They are coming. I can hear their song...'

Bakhariel is facing back down the buried road we have come from. At the edge of sight, I can see the eyes of the humans watching, wide and fearful.

'Can you not hear their song?' croaks Bakhariel.

I see the firelight coming down the broken road between the pillars. There are figures running ahead of the blaze. Human figures, or figures that were once human. They are burning. Red and yellow and pink flames spill from them. Their skin and sinew is charring on their bones, their mouths open wide as theirs lips burn back from their teeth. Their cries echo off the walls. They are not calling out in pain. They are calling out in exultation, in agony, in joy and hunger. You see, even here in the underworld of the Palace there are those who let the powers of the warp fill the cracks in their soul. Tonight all of the poison in their dreams has come to answer their prayers. The daemons that have come with the storms have poured into them and now are loose, and hungry. They are not coming for us, though, they are coming for the crowds of mortals who are about to begin screaming. We are just here by chance.

I look at the tide of manifesting daemons, flooding my

sight with flame-light. I can see teeth lengthening, flesh twist-ing into new shapes, fingers becoming claws. I should go. I should let this play out, and keep on towards the goal that I have waited so long to reach. I should not do what I already know I must.

My guns are in my hands. Bolt shells punch through burning flesh. Plasma explodes through fanged mouths. And I am going towards the burning tide of possessed souls, and my words call my brothers with me.

'Angels of Caliban, with me!'

At my word, they follow, all of them: the old and bitter knights, betrayers and breakers of oaths, the tainted and the broken. Part of me fancies that if I were to turn and look at them in that moment I might see them as they were, proud warriors clad in armour, with skill of sword, and will and strength enough to break an empire. I fancy that I might see my brothers and remember again who I am.

Our charge hits home. Claws meet blades. Gunfire rips into flesh. I fire into a thing with a face of stretched skin and teeth. Its skull vanishes. Bone claws rake my right shoulder. I fire without looking and the daemon falls. Flesh burns to black slime. My pistols speak as I move, weaving explosions and sun-bright fire amongst the mass of distorting faces. I put a burst of plasma through the open jaws of a creature. The energy burns through the back of its skull and lances through the thing behind it. Coolant vents from the pistol.

I spin my pistols high, reloading without pause. Another creature comes at me with claws that were fingers. I kick it back. It lands and springs at me again, arms reaching, skull cracking as it spreads its jaws wide.

I blow its head to bits.

Then I am moving again, weaving my own song amongst

the tide. My pistols shake in my grasp, and the world is a stuttered blur of muzzle flash. I see the tide of daemons breaking over knights in black armour. I see their swords turn claws and maces shatter limbs.

A tentacle whips from the edge of sight. I begin to turn, but it wraps around my plasma pistol and up my arm. One of the daemon things has me. The body that it took was old, and dying, but it has poured unnatural strength into the withered frame. Cords of muscle twist under translucent skin, purple and writhing. Its lower jaw is hanging off its face. Tiny hands reach from its throat. It is smiling with a second mouth that spreads across its forehead. Its left arm is a soft rope of stretched skin and flesh, and it's that limb which is binding my arm. Its other hand is burning. Cooking meat falls from fingers that are growing into talons.

The tentacle tightens. Spines grow from it as it squeezes. I feel the tips punch through my armour and into my flesh. Venom flows into my blood. It burns… It is not a mortal thing. Its poison is born of the warp, of lost dreams and burnt hopes.

The venom feels…

It feels like the sweetness of sugar and the comfort of sleep.

'Come to us at lasssttt, divided son,' croons the daemon. *'The lassst inch to fall is the sssweetessst…'*

I am floating. I am falling. I want to let go. Colours swirl in place of sight. I feel the brighter angel of my soul dimming. I feel the call to give in fully, to be what others fear I am: a creature of Chaos, a slave to darkness, irredeemable, forsaken. But then, even as light fades, the Dark Angel within, the thing bound in bitterness and vengeance and rage, speaks.

'No!' I shout the word aloud. I fire without looking, but my shots land true. The tentacle releases. The barbs pull from my flesh, and the whisper of the venom fades. Sight slams back into my eyes. A thing of squirming suppleness writhes at my feet. It is bleeding black smoke and blood froth. It gasps at me with a mouth that has no tongue.

I shoot it in its needle smile. About me the daemon tide is dissolving, the fires within their stolen flesh guttering. I turn and look into the dark where the mortals were. Most have fled, but there are still a few, frozen with awe and terror. I cross my guns over my chest and bow my head to them. I wonder if any of them will survive to remember this night, to remember me. I hope so.

'Lord Cypher,' calls Korlael. 'We must move swiftly if we are to reach the door.'

'Yes, we must,' I reply, and then call to the rest of my followers. 'Battle is done, brothers, follow fast.' I holster my pistols and turn back to the dark of the way we were travelling. The others do the same, reloading, sheathing swords, holstering weapons.

'Here...' hisses Bakhariel. He has not moved. He is turned away from us, looking back to where the light of the daemon fire first came from. His shoulders are rising and falling as though he is struggling to breathe. 'Here... they...'

This is not the first time Brother Bakhariel has had such moments. His broken soul has ever struggled to keep itself true, and this night has been like no other. The power of the Dark Gods waxes and the cracks in Bakhariel's soul are splitting wide.

'The Neverborn are gone, Bakhariel,' says Korlael, 'and so must we be. Come...'

Korlael reaches forwards to pull our brother with us.

Bakhariel smashes his fist out. The blow sends Korlael spinning through the air. The instant slows, becomes eternal.

A storm charge is in the air, heavy and rank. Sparks are playing over Bakhariel as he turns. His eyes are pits of blue flame. Molten fire is running from his speaker-grille. The armour of his helm is cracking with heat.

Bakhariel... poor Bakhariel. The cup of his damnation was always going to overrun. Perhaps it is the warp storms breaking across Terra. Perhaps it is the call of the gods he gave his soul to. Perhaps it is just his time.

My failing. I have let him rot for too long. I knew it would come to this, but can you forgive me for wanting my brother at my side just a little longer? Can you understand my not wanting to judge him for his weakness?

No matter. It is too late now.

'You shall burn,' roars a daemonic voice using Bakhariel's mouth. *'You shall be ashes. You shall be ours.'*

The daemon in Bakhariel throws him forwards at us. His armour cracks. Flesh and fire pour out through the fissures. His fingers are extending to talons. Shadow and pyre light billow around him.

Namaer is the first to die. Bakhariel's claws punch through his brother's chest and head in a single blow. Namaer's body flashes to blood-steam and smoke. Bakhariel casts the empty armour aside, and judders forwards. His eyes are swirls of fire and silver smoke, and they are fixed on me. I can feel the hunger in them and the anger. So long have I resisted the embrace of the Neverborn. I am a warrior who stands with one foot in night and another in sunlight. And both light and dark hunger for what they cannot have.

'You are ours, Cypher. Willing or unwilling, you are ours,' shouts the daemon inside my brother. *'You will not reach the redemption you seek. There is no vengeance for you to reap. You fall here.'*

The bloated, burning form of Bakhariel strikes me. The blow is not a killing blow, just enough to crack my breastplate and send me down to the floor. It wants to toy with me. They are like that, the Neverborn, they like to play with the things they covet. And me? Why did I not shoot? Why did I let myself be struck? I am not certain. Guilt at what I have done and not done? Hope that this does not have to end as I know it must?

'Cypher… Cypher…'

The daemon looms above me. Bakhariel's armour is flowing like wax. Muscle fibres are forming from armour plates. Ghost light is boiling off him. Particles of shattered stone and debris from the floor are rising to orbit his form. The daemon puts a foot that is now a hoof on the broken armour of my chest, and smiles down at me with lips made from molten steel.

'Cypher… the warrior with no name… the soul divided… What pleasure shall be yours, what slaughter? Your quest is over, fool knight. The only vengeance is ours, and the only redemption lies in our embrace.'

Daemons. There was a time when they did not exist. There was a time when to use a word like 'daemon' would have betrayed a naivete about the nature of the universe. There were no gods in that age. No daemons. Just entities, and properties of reality that we did not understand. Now that seems naive. Daemons are real. The Dark Gods are real. Chaos is real. We can dispute the names. We can say that the words 'god' and 'daemon' are only the words humanity has to express the powers of the warp. We can say that we are projecting, that the idea of gods and infernal monsters comes from our ancient past, an old fiction sewn onto a current horror. We might have a point on all these counts. That does not stop them being real.

The warp is another dimension. It is not distant. It is right here, the width of a wish away from the physical reality we see and feel. It is there in the weight of your foot as it rests on the floor. It is there in the air as it passes your lips. It is there in the fall of sunlight into shadow. It is a dimension not of matter, but of thought and psychic energy. Vast and terrible energy. It is the realm of the soul, of dreams and ideas. Laughter and hope live in its depths, rage sends red storms through it. The only law that exists within its bounds is the law of dreams. All of the thoughts of every living thing gather in the warp. Our fear and desire and spite form its tides, our cowardice and bravery salt its depths. It is both springhead and sump for sentience.

What of the Dark Gods, you ask? What of daemons? The answer is simple. They are the warp. Just as you cannot separate the storm from the sea, the Dark Gods are the warp. They are all of the darkness of sentience run together, churning the depths. If you like, you could think of them as vast, stable whirlpools in the sea of souls. The thoughts, actions and emotions of all creatures that live or have ever lived feed them. They are eternal, waveforms created by life, which never break or fade but run on without beginning or end.

Why do we call them gods? Why do some worship them, and call out to them for vengeance and reward? Because humans have always thought to placate things they fear and things they do not understand. Here on Terra, in times long forgotten, sailors would pour blood into storm waters in the hope that it would calm the anger of the sea. In a way, the cultist who places their bloody tribute on an altar is no different. The difference is that the ancient seas did not answer those who poured blood into the water. The Dark Gods do answer.

You see, the Dark Gods are not sentient. They are *made*

of sentience. They desire and reach and hunger and corrupt because that is what we do. They are not beings as we would think of them. They destroy, and torment, and tempt because that is what they are made of – just as a sword-edge cuts, they corrupt. They hunger for the reality that spawned them, you see. They are life's eternal nightmares trying to live in the waking world. What of the daemons, you ask? The daemons *are* the Dark Gods. They are pieces of the great storm, extrusions of the power of Rage, or Change, or Despair as they exist in the warp. They are ideas and emotions left to fester and grow skins from all our fears. They come when summoned, or when they can slip through a crack in reality, or when a mind offers them a nest in which to grow. They have no thoughts or emotions, not really. They are simply power and driving instinct. Those instincts may be subtle or crude – seduction or slaughter – but they pursue them just as a shark pursues the scent of blood. Because it is their nature.

We were right, in a way. There are no such things as gods or daemons. They are just us, the mirror to our souls and the darkness of our lives. That does not stop them being real, though.

'Bakhariel, no!' It is Korlael, and he runs towards us as he shouts. Blood is pouring from a gouge in his chestplate, but still he comes. Even though Bakhariel is now little more than a shape wrapped around the power of the warp, still Korlael wants to pull his brother back from the abyss he is falling into.

'Darkness at noon…' calls the daemon that possesses Bakhariel. *'Fire at midnight…'*

But the possibility of salvation is a fraying thread, and there is not much of Bakhariel left to grasp it. Maybe if Bakhariel had listened to Korlael all those years ago; maybe if I had not let him off the leash; maybe… But what is done is done, and what is about to happen is far beyond my control.

The daemon that was Bakhariel reaches down to me. The air burns in front of its talons.

'Forgive me!' shouts Korlael, and his sword cleaves into Bakhariel's back.

The daemon rears back, twisting in pain, as Korlael wrenches his sword free. It turns. Bakhariel's spine breaks as the daemon's body swells with rage. The shape of his armour is just visible inside the furnace glare burning from within. It looms above Korlael, bleeding ash from the wound he gave it.

'You shall end here!' it roars.

I am on my feet. My pistols are in my hands. The eyes of my other brothers are turning towards me, but they have not moved. Perhaps some of them wish me to fall now, or die, or are frozen by the sight of what is happening.

I do not pause. I fire. Bakhariel and the daemon within him bellow with pain. The first shots blow out the backs of the daemon's legs and vaporise the flesh of its arms. The next shots are a deluge that rip into its mass. Black blood scatters in the air, burning as it falls. I fire until my pistols are dry. Both daemon and Space Marine should be dead; it still has rage enough to live.

'You!' It turns on Korlael, its body reknitting as it moves.

'I am sorry, brother,' says Korlael, and his sword punches through it from front to back.

The daemon staggers, an arm's length of steel projecting from its chest. Then Korlael rips the sword up and out of its back. Flesh and blood and fire and ash arc through the air. I watch as the daemon flees the husk that is Bakhariel. There is real blood falling from his body now, and in the ruin of his head I can see human eyes.

'Brother...' gasps Bakhariel as he sees me. It is the clearest word I have heard Bakhariel speak in decades. Gone are the ravings of one touched by gods and bound to nightmares. 'Brother...'

I reload my bolt pistol.

'Please.'

I fire once into his skull. Then twice more into the mass of flesh and broken armour as it collapses to the floor. The remnants of the daemon drain from the broken shell of meat that was Bakhariel. I look at it for a second. It is a pitiful thing, but then aren't we all in death?

'You are injured, lord,' says Korlael. I do not reply. I holster my guns and start off again into the dark. It was always going to be this way. I call behind me as I move.

'The door waits for us,' I say.

My remaining brothers follow in silence.

FOURTEEN

The Imperial Palace

Cradus watches the Custodes grav-tank cut through the streets of the Inner Palace. It is a golden dart, slicing through the labyrinth of buildings. Nothing tries to slow or stop it and it switches routes around riots, fires and debris like its pilot can see through stone. In a sense he can. The Custodians' keep taps into every data-system in the Palace. They have cogitator temples and servitor farms that sift that data, spindle and shape it into a unified vision. They see the arbitrators die as rockets hit the bridge they are standing on. They hear the panicked vox-calls as a blaze reaches a power conduit hub. They see the flash of an explosion on the horizon caught in the eye of watch-servitors. Even on this night, the eyes of the Custodians see and guide the grav-tank through the chaos.

Cradus is watching the grav-tank from the belly of a small

aircraft. It's a dagger, carbon-black. It's angular, razor-edged, made to cut through auspex, and its wings beat the air with a hushed thrum. Cradus lies flat on his belly to steer it. A sensor cradle presses against his face. The world is green under his eyes. Behind him, curled in the craft's tiny cargo space is Kestra. She is Vindicare. A killer of the Ninth Degree in the art of her temple. The other members of the Court have sent her to ensure that the execution of the target is complete. Some of the temples might consider that an insult, but Cradus understands. He has killed Chapter Masters of the Adeptus Astartes, and ended the ambitions of alien warlords. He has taught the craft of death to apprentices and mastered forty of its greater arts. He is of the Twenty-Sixth Degree, Omega-level. He is marked to head the Callidus one day, and perhaps even take the seat of Grand Master. He is old in murder and years, and knows that in hunting me he is hunting no mundane target.

He watches as the grav-tank passes through a security cordon and slows as it readies to halt. He configures a vox-thief with his fingertips then presses the transmission trigger.

'Warden Hekkarron,' he says. He knows that the Custodian will recognise his voice. 'We are in your shadow. We have the sword. We will follow.'

No reply comes, but Cradus knows Hekkarron heard. He watches the grav-tank as its hatch opens, and the black-and-gold figure within dismounts. Bird-skull servo-units scatter from the craft's belly. Each is no bigger than the tip of a human thumb. They lock onto Hekkarron and begin to track him. The Custodian will not sense them. They have been engineered to mesh with the sensors in his armour.

Cradus brings the aircraft around. Its wings beat the air as it comes to a hover and then folds into the rooftops with a whisper. He releases the hatch and dismounts. Kestra follows without a word. The pair begin to move, two shadows amongst shadows.

The Imperium is a carrion kingdom. It lives only so long as it eats the corpses and souls of its people. Some it chews in the teeth of iron cogs. Some it swallows down with the thunder of shells and the blaze of gunfire. Some it keeps alive so that it can feed on their strength. That is the truth. That is the Imperium, and the Emperor, who sits locked into a device of torment at its heart, knows it and can do nothing to stop it. Beneath the skin of gold there is a skull.

You don't believe me? Let me show you.

A boy was born on a world circling a distant star. It was a world of forests and oceans and distant mountains capped with snow. The boy was not born high, or low, but to a family that cared for him. He knew affection and laughter and tears. He had two sisters and a younger brother who followed him like a shadow. When he should have been sleeping, the boy would sneak out to run on the sand of the shore at night. The smell of salt spray and the sound of breaking waves haunt the dreams that are all that is left of that time to him now.

No war came. That would be later, and when its fires sent smoke to cover the sun, the boy would not be a boy, or even a man, and he would be long gone from his home. What came in the end was the ship. Black and vast, hanging above the sea, like a mountain cut loose of its roots and hauled up into the sky to hide the sun. Terror came with it, terror and the figures in red robes, and burnished armour, and cloaks of pale fur. There had been stories of the witch seekers who came in the Black Ships, but they had never come in living memory.

Blind creatures ran through the streets sniffing for souls. People were rounded up, tested, divided. Some were killed.

Some were let go. Some were taken up into the ships, chained, heads clamped in cold iron and rune-etched silver.

The boy was not taken at first. He did not try to run. His family did not know that he could call the wind with a wish or hear their joy and anger. They did not know he was a witch, and he did not know either. The seekers knew though, and they found him. Blind jackals scented his soul, and the soldiers surrounded his house. They took him. What happened to his family? Do you think they were treated with kindness? Do you believe that mercy was shown? Maybe. But I have never known or seen true mercy in this universe.

The boy went on, chained in darkness as the ship crossed the stars. There was pain of every kind in that ship. He was one amongst many, all of them psykers harvested from humanity. He was evaluated and found to be strong, very strong, not just in power but in body and will. That earned him more pain but a degree of protection. They were long years, those years crossing the stars, but at last, older and half-broken, he arrived at Terra.

You must imagine it – tides of humanity chained and bound by psychic inhibitors, goaded from the bellies of Black Ships into the mouth of the Hollow Mountain. Thousands of them, tens of thousands every day. Today. Here at the heart of the Imperium, this happens. Some go to the halls of the astropaths, their souls strong but not strong enough. They will see the Emperor who is their god and give their eyes to that moment. Most of the rest go to the Golden Throne. Old men and young, weeping, unconscious or grimly defiant. They live as brief flames, their souls and their power burning to nothing as they add to the pyre that people think keeps the Emperor alive. Tens of thousands every day, life turned to dust, thoughts reduced to silent screams that howl around the heart of the Palace.

The flames were not the fate of the boy, though he saw and

felt what was happening. He was following a different path, a very narrow path, open to only a few. He was given to the Scholastica Psykana. Terra became his home as adepts in silver masks assessed him again. He passed through the first gate of this path, and the tests became training. He began to live half in dreams and half in waking, and found that he could take one and make it the other. The memories of seashore and spray faded, and always in the present there were the ghost screams of the souls fed to the Golden Throne.

He excelled in his training. He could twist an iron bar into a knot with a thought, and ink script with a quill held only by will. Three years after he came to Terra, his tutors took him to see the tides of his fellow psykers pass into the mouth of the Golden Throne. He was not even a man yet, but his soul was old already. He had become an aspirant of the Psykana. He walked the roads and halls of the Imperial Palace many times at the side of his masters and mistresses. One day he sensed a stone statue falling from the wall of a high cathedral as he passed beneath its walls. He sprang aside and pushed his fellows out of the way. The statue crushed a pilgrim lighting a candle at the foot of the wall.

The Psykana instructors took note and new tests were applied to the boy. His body was now tested as much as his mind. He was loosed in warrens of the Palace where the feral servitors and mutant vermin lurk. He was not alone at first, but his companions did not last long; they died through mischance or from slowness or on rusted claws that came from the dark.

The boy lived. He killed. He learned to read the currents of the stagnant air as it rushes through the layers of old streets and buildings crushed by the weight of the Palace above. He learned the truths and secrets that are there to be heard if you live in the forgotten gaps of the Palace. His psychic powers became sharper, and he learned to live with the howl of the dead that filled the quiet in his skull.

He did not survive; he thrived, and all the while he was watched by giants in the dark, skull-helmed figures who he sometimes glimpsed but never approached. Then, at last, they came for him, his instructors from the Scholastica and the death-faced giants. He did not try to escape. He should have, but he did not. They took him. He was to be submitted into the process of becoming one of the Adeptus Astartes, a gift given from the Adeptus Astra Telepathica to the Space Marines by ancient pact. The Chapter of Space Marines that he was bound for was decided by no other factor than that they were the next Chapter marked as receiving one of the prime harvest of psykers. The boy would go far away from Terra, and be remade in body as well as mind. He would learn terrible secrets and the craft of war.

He would become a Dark Angel…

Catacombs

Decades later, Mordachi, Epistolary of the Dark Angels Librarius, moves through the deep tunnels of the Palace he never thought he would return to. Things with fur and dozens of legs skitter out of their way. Water drips into the quiet. Niches of bones line the walls. The long stems of pale fungus jut from the eye sockets of skulls. The glow of the Dark Angels' eyepieces catches spores breathing from the fungal blooms. These places have not seen light for a hundred years.

'Why the Throne Room, Brother-Librarian?' asks Nariel.

'I do not know,' replies Mordachi.

'He cannot hope to reach it and live.'

'He has come this far.'

'The Custodians–'

'This is a night on which the immaterium screams, a lost son of the Emperor returns to the Throneworld, and the fires of war burn within the Palace itself. If there is any time when the Emperor's protectors might fail, it is this night.'

'What else did the Fallen reveal to you?'

'Nothing more than I have said. Cypher seeks to breach the Inner Sanctum. He believes he has a way that will be open, a door left unguarded.'

Mordachi falls silent, and Nariel does not press the question. Mordachi knows that Nariel does not wholly believe him. Doubt and secrets – that has ever been our order's curse. The sons of the Lion never speak in whole truths, and we never trust fully. That has cost us much, but if you want me to tell you the truth – I think there is a virtue in distrust.

'What is our mission now, brother?' asks Nariel at last.

'Our purpose remains unchanged. Cypher and the Fallen cannot be allowed to escape, and no one must know who they are. No matter the cost.'

They go on through the dark, down, and then up, climbing broken stairs until they reach the place they are looking for, the place that Azkhar told Mordachi about – the way into the Inner Sanctum. They hush as they approach.

I walk in the deep dark of the Palace, too. Terra's forgotten past is the dust stirred by my feet. I turn a corner and see the door. I stop for a second. The door waits for me. The way to it is dark before us. The passage is stone. The air is quiet apart from the hum of our armour and the sound of my steps. My brothers and I move without speaking. We are about to pass from the Outer Palace to the Inner Sanctum, to the last city-within-a-city. It is dark; even to my eyes this is a place of shadows. I can see the beginning of the end now, just there, at the end of this corridor.

The Path of Martyrs

Hekkarron steps onto the Path of Martyrs. He has his spear in hand. The light falling through the high windows above is from a handful of ancient lumen plates, set behind and diluted by dust-covered glass. The path is more a passage, long and narrow. Two tanks could not pass each other here. The ceiling is hundreds of yards tall. The faces of huge statues look down from niches through spiderweb veils. They are vast. It is said that once, in the Age of Apostasy, nine thousand souls gave their lives trying to hold back the forces of Goge Vandire from the Inner Sanctum. It's not true. Goge Vandire was a fool, but even he was not fool enough to try and breach the Inner Sanctum of the Palace by force. No blood was spilled here then. The deaths and martyrdom on this spot came before that, long before, in a war that almost all who fought in it have forgotten. All except me.

As Hekkarron moves, the gold and black of his armour merge, and he seems to be one of the shadows of the statues that loom above. He is silent. The Assassins Cradus and Kestra are there in the dark, lost even to his senses.

He can see the figure in the shadows at the far end of the colonnade. The figure is approaching the doors at the end of the rows of statues. The doors are sealed, bound with chains and bolts that were set six thousand years before, and have never been loosed since. This is a discarded and sealed way into the Sanctum beyond. The Custodians watch it, but tonight they are thousands of miles away facing the daemons of the warp. All except one.

Hekkarron pauses. There is something wrong. His senses can feel it. But he keeps moving.

I stop on the threshold at the end of the dark passage. The way through, the next step, is just there beyond the door. My hands go to my guns, my fingers resting on the polished pla-steel and ivory. Am I really here? Have I truly succeeded in coming this far?

Hekkarron's eyes catch the shape of a shadow within a shadow. The systems in his helm and his genhanced vision latch on to the shape and peel back the dark. He sees the lines of armour, of weapons, of a tattered robe laid over it like a shroud.

His senses – far keener than even a Space Marine's – detect the buzz of active power armour and the beat of twin hearts. There are others, too, folded into the shadows. He can hear the silence of the guns in their hands, and the breath held in lungs as they watch him. This will be bloody, but after all, isn't that how everything ends?

'It is over,' says Hekkarron. He steps forward, towards the figure in the shadows. His grip on his guardian spear is light. He has not ignited it yet. His mind has sifted his senses and he already knows how the first instants of slaughter will play out. 'You shall not pass this door. It will cost your life. I would offer you survival, a life in chains, but after all you have done to get here, I do not think you will give up freedom even at the cost of death.'

He pauses, watching the figure in the shadows, listening to the held breaths and the hearts beating in the dark.

'There is one thing I would know, though – why?'

In truth, he does want an answer to the question, but that is not why he asked. He is waiting for the Assassins that have followed him here to settle into place. He knows they are there.

Hekkarron sees the figure step from the dark, hears the tensing of fingers on triggers... And he knows something is wrong. A shift in the hum of the power armour, a detail in the figure's stance. Now he senses again the pressure on his mind. He realises that something has hidden the truth from his eyes. For an instant he wishes that he had not left Ancia on that platform far away. He wishes that he had predicted something that he could never have predicted.

He sees Mordachi in the dark, with a sword in his hand. Mordachi senses the recognition in the Custodian. Neither of them have any choice now. He feels for the first time what other mortals feel when the universe decides that they are a plaything of fools. He feels crushed by reality.

Do you want me to explain what has happened, and how this came about? Mordachi is here because he believes that this is the way I will come. He believes that because that is what Azkhar told him. Azkhar believed that because I told him. They should have known better, shouldn't they? Hekkarron and the Assassins are here because of the vision that Ancia had of my thoughts while I was in the Dark Cells. They all believe they will find me here, and they believe it because, by one means or another, I told them. As I said, they should have known better.

'It is not Cypher, this is not the target! You have deceived us, Custodian!' Hekkarron hears the hiss of the Assassin, Cradus, in his ears.

It is not much, but it is enough to make the Custodian hesitate.

Mordachi does not hesitate. His course is already set, his oaths and the secrets of his Chapter enough that this loyal son of the Imperium will kill one of the Emperor's own without pause.

Mordachi raises his gun and fires, and Hekkarron is moving, but a sliver of time too late. His guardian spear is lit with lightning. But he is alone.

And that is how demigods die. They die alone.

FIFTEEN

Forgotten Doorway

Far below the Path of Martyrs, I put my hand on the old door. Its metal is corroded, but still strong. I look around at my brothers. Korlael moves forwards. The flame-light of the torch finds the old carvings and the worn faces carved into the stone of the door's setting. Like so much, it has been forgotten. How can a way, even a small way, into the heart of the greatest fortress in the Imperium be forgotten? The same way anything can – you just have to wait.

'The key, my lord.' Korlael holds out the key that I entrusted him with three centuries ago. The key that hung on his armour with a dozen others that mean nothing. I take it from him, and slot it into the hole in the door. I turn it. It resists for a second, and then cogs and bolts in the door release with a clang.

I pause. I never doubted that I would get here, but still its reality makes me hesitate. Beyond this layer of rusted steel lies the Inner Sanctum, and at the heart of this final city the Emperor who made me.

I push the door open. There is light. Not much, just a thin strain of pale light falling from somewhere high above and far away. The air that breathes through the door smells of dust... dust and the past.

Did you ever doubt that I would reach here? After so long, it must surely be inevitable. All journeys must end, no matter where the road leads.

'My lord?' asks Korlael. 'Is something wrong?'

I look around at him, and at my Fallen brothers that have followed me this far. I think I smile, then I step through the door.

The Path of Martyrs

Have you ever seen a Custodian fight Space Marines? Some say that it is like watching a lion fight wolves. There is insight in that, but it does not capture the whole truth.

There are ten Dark Angels with Mordachi in the dark of the Path of Martyrs. All of them are veterans, inductees of the Inner Circle, the elite. They are masters of war and killing. They move as a seamless whole, fearless, devastating, lethal.

Gunfire carves the dark into fire-orange tatters. Explosions roll thunder up to the ceiling high above. In that roar, the sound of Hekkarron's grunt of effort is lost. The snap of his guardian spear's lightning a hiss lost to the deluge. He is the target of fire from Space Marines in prepared positions, with angles of fire, cover and elevation. He is as good as dead.

Except he's not. He's moving.

'Sustain fire!' shouts Nariel.

Hekkarron reaches one of the Dark Angels. Just like that he is there. Explosions shatter against armour, and send black and golden shards scattering with the shrapnel. The explosive impacts would be enough to pulp a human inside their armour. They stagger Hekkarron, but that's all. A lion. Almost right.

The edge of the guardian spear takes a Dark Angel in the throat. It's a single-blow kill, chosen so that it does not interrupt Hekkarron's charge. He is amongst them now, in the spaces and shadows at the feet of the statues. A golden blur. His guardian spear an arc of glinting steel and lightning. Another two Dark Angels are already dead at his feet. He is taller than them, his bulk greater, but he moves like the breath of a storm wind.

'Bring him down!' shouts Mordachi into the vox.

Hekkarron kills another, slicing through the warrior's torso from waist to shoulder, and he is still moving, turning, pulling away from the firing angles of the rest even as they try to bring their guns to bear. The blood of the first Dark Angel to die is still falling, a mist in the air, when he kills the fourth.

No, not a lion. A lightning bolt.

Another blow, another perfect cut that tears ceramite and flesh apart.

One of the Dark Angels takes a step back, brings the barrel of his plasma gun up. Hekkarron thrusts his spear out, the haft running through his fingers to its heel. The spear tip punches through the Space Marine's finger and slices it from his hand before he can pull the trigger of his gun.

Hekkarron sweeps the spear up before its weight can drop and whirls it in an arc. The blade slices into another of the Dark Angels, through helm and into skull. The Dark Angel with the plasma gun has already switched the gun to his other hand without pause, ready to fire. Hekkarron spins his spear so that it is in both his hands and triggers the gun mounted beneath the blade head. Fire blasts into the Dark Angel's weapon.

Plasma explodes out of the ruin of the gun. The Dark Angel dissolves, a blur of ash and ceramite dust in a starburst.

Six. Custodian Warden Hekkarron has killed six of the Dark Angels in the time it takes a human heart to beat as many times. Remarkable. You cannot help but admire that degree of lethality. I admire it. The Custodians are a breed apart from humanity and the Space Marines. The sharp edge of mankind refined. A tyrant-genius' idea of perfection.

'Clear back from him!' shouts Mordachi.

And you know what has to happen to something that is perfect.

'Clear!' calls Nariel.

You have been paying attention, haven't you?

'Now!'

The surviving Dark Angels that are close to Hekkarron leap clear. A storm of lightning and telekinetic force breaks over the Custodian. Threads of white light bore into black-and-gold armour; invisible ropes enfold limbs, tighten, squeeze.

Hekkarron keeps moving, straining against the power that is strangling and burning him. His mind and body are more than just his flesh and thought. His armour more than gold. Alchemy and stolen fire run through his veins. His will is adamant. Ancient words etch the inside of his armour, woven with the letters of his name. Frost is forming on him and the stones beneath his feet. The air shivers. Mordachi is pouring all his will into this. He feels blood vessels burst in his own throat and skull. The world is dimming before his eyes. Hekkarron slows, but he will never stop. He is not me, or one of my Fallen brothers. He is not so weak.

But this is not just a battle of spirit, and Mordachi does not need to stop Hekkarron. He just needs to give his brothers the seconds they need to aim and fire.

Two missiles streak from the sides of the Path of Martyrs. They strike Hekkarron. A great pall of flame and dust and broken stone punches up to the ceiling high above. Helm and auto-targeters lock onto Hekkarron's last position. Bolters fire into the dust cloud.

The silence that follows feels like the striking of a great bell.

Mordachi keeps his psychic grip on Hekkarron for a moment longer, then releases it. He staggers against the plinth of one of the statues.

'Brother-Librarian?' asks Nariel.

Mordachi does not move for a moment. Within his armour he is shaking. Blood is clotting on the inside of his helm. The howls of the Golden Throne feel louder, sharper. His flesh is fever-hot. Inside his mind, the enormity of what they have just done and the effort it took is a cold abyss at the core of his thoughts. He feels empty. That is as it should be. What else should be the price of breaking something perfect?

'Deal with our dead, sergeant,' he says to Nariel. 'We have no time to wait.'

'And Cypher?'

'This was his doing. He has found another way into the Sanctum and used us and his hunters to end each other. We must find him before... before...'

He can't bring himself to say what he fears I intend. He turns his back as Nariel and the survivors go to each of their dead brothers. The devotions they speak are brief. They lock and arm a plasma grenade to each. No precious gene-seed will be taken from these dead warriors. They will go to the flames to keep the secrets of their Chapter and the shame of our Legion.

Then the Dark Angels leave in silence, passing within the Inner Sanctum through the door they thought I would use. I am not done with them yet. They must pay for their sins, as do we all, but for now they are free. Behind them the charges detonate. Fire consumes the corpses.

High above, unseen in the shadows, the Assassins watch and follow. Why did they not intervene? Because they are the most precise kind of murderers in existence. They are there to hunt and kill me. I was not there, and so they watched. If you think that they were on the same side as Hekkarron then you are deluded. There is no unity of purpose in the Imperium and there is less in its ancient heart.

Hekkarron's Mindscape

The golden warrior falls in fire.

'By the light of eternity do I serve... By the will of illumination am I made...'

He speaks the words of his oaths as he falls.

'By the strength of my will no enemy shall pass within sight of the Throne...'

He is dying. He is fighting to live.

'My sword shall break...'

In one world he is lying on the tiled floor of the Path of Martyrs. Blood, deep red and laced with ancient secrets and divinity, pooling from broken armour. Eyes closed within a cloven helm.

'My spear shall shatter...'

In another world, he is a burning comet falling through a red sky. Beneath him ripples a black sea. Islands of cold rock rise from the spray, jagged peaks growing into the air to greet him.

'But I shall not fail…'

Which is more real – the bloody truth or the dream of burning?

'I shall not fall.'

In the world within, the dark sea grows beneath him until it fills his eyes. Wind rushes past.

'I shall stand eternal guard.'

He strikes water. It is black. He is sightless. Not even the light of the sky he fell from reaches him. Cold pours into him. He is drowning, and as the water fills his lungs he can hear a voice inside his ear.

'You have failed.'

It is the voice of the Assassin, Cradus. Hekkarron tries to answer, tries to breathe, but in the world where he could breathe, his lungs and throat are already filling with blood, and here in the un-world he only sinks deeper.

You may be wondering if this is real, or a vision, and if it is either, then what place it has in my story. But I told you before; this is not my story. And besides, where can a tale of mysteries and destinies lead but into the world of dreams and visions?

'All those years and decades of service…' says the Assassin's voice. *'All the seconds and minutes of your rare life, Hekkarron, and you fail at the one thing that you were created to do.'*

Are you listening? You wanted the truth, but can you tell that truth from a lie?

'You let the one called Cypher loose. You let him slip through your grasp. You let yourself believe you could catch him. But you have failed and now Cypher goes to slay the Emperor.'

Is that what you were expecting?

'He can do it too. He has the will and shall have the means.'

Do I? Do I have the means to kill my creator? You know… I think I might.

'*Cypher is death walking into the place that you exist to keep sacrosanct,*' says the voice of Cradus. '*He is the doom of the light that shines at the heart of mankind. On this night, when the tides of Chaos break over the heart of the Imperium, when warriors and soldiers hold back that storm, you have let the death of all pass like a pilgrim through the gates you guard.*'

Hekkarron can hear the voice, and the words seep into him like the cold of the water he sinks through. His kind are not given to despair; it is a gift withheld from them, but in this endless night, Hekkarron knows the pain that comes only from failing and knowing you have failed. He sinks deeper, while in a different world his rare blood is flowing from his wounds faster than it can clot.

Then from far above through the black water he hears another voice.

'Hekkarron...'

He can almost grasp it, but then it is gone.

SIXTEEN

Inner Sanctum, Bridge of Ascension

The Dark Angels come to the Bridge of Ascension. The Emperor was said to have been borne across it on His procession to the Golden Throne. All lies, all dreams by those who create the myths by which power persists. The Emperor was not dragged across these stones, bloody and slipping into death. That was another place, but this bridge still matters, and it matters for a very simple reason – once you cross it, only the ultimate doors stand between you and the Emperor Himself. There are no guards, just the drop, and the great abyss beneath and the statue-covered cliffs to either side. Here the corpse light dances across the stone faces and crackles in the air. False winds howl and murmur. It is snowing. Frost conjuring from nothing and melting to smoke.

So close. So very, very close. I have come to the threshold.

What? Did you think a simple key in a door and I would be in the presence of my maker? No, that door was just the way into this place, into the Inner Sanctum, and while I have outwitted our enemies, I have not outrun them. So, here on this bridge I turn and face those who hunt us.

A figure in black armour and caul waits for the Dark Angels on the bridge. A sword hangs on his back. Mordachi goes forwards, his brothers spread into the statues and balconies on the walls either side of the bridge. The Librarian has his sword in his hand. Its edge is lit with psy-fire. His mind is shrieking with pain, the throb of the presence of the Golden Throne a hammer striking the inside of his skull. He sees the figure waiting for him and the first thing that strikes him is the arrogance of such an act – to wait for your hunters, blade bare, unmoving. He knows it is probably a trap, but he slows. He waits a heartbeat for a shot that does not come. He comes forwards, cautious. He should turn back, but he keeps coming. You see he is a Dark Angel, and so he thinks he wants the truth. The shrouded figure on the bridge speaks before he can ask a question.

'What did you do with them?' asks the figure.

Mordachi stops at the question.

'Your brothers that died this night – what did you do with them?'

'Their fate and end was your doing, Fallen One,' replies Mordachi.

'Fallen…' says the figure, and there is a sneer in the word. 'Fallen… Look at yourself! We were knights, we were the first warriors of the Imperium. We were Angels. What of that remains in you?'

'I am sorry.'

'Your sorrow is just a shroud for your hypocrisy.'

'I am sorry that my dead brothers had to bear the burden of your guilt,' says Mordachi. 'Your kind dragged our order and our honour into the abyss.'

'And what of the honour of honesty? Which of us comes here cloaked in shadows?'

'We are what your betrayal forced us to become. Do you think that we crave dishonour? Do you imagine we are ignorant of what our deeds make us? You can stop this, Cypher. You can stop this all. You can have peace. Submit, confess, repent. It will all end, for you, for those that follow you, for us all.'

The figure on the bridge points at Mordachi with his sword. 'And you? Will you kneel? Will you beg forgiveness from the dead of Caliban?'

'So we stand where we began,' says Mordachi and shakes his head, disappointed but not surprised.

'Just so.'

'That brings me sorrow.'

'It shouldn't. It was and is always this way.'

They look at each other then, but Mordachi still does not realise it is not me that he is talking to.

High above the bridge, the Assassin Cradus crouches in the dark. The hunched back and age-worn body that he wore in the Court of Assassins are gone. Now he is a shape of night-skinned muscle, feline in grace, coiled in shadow. He bears a sword on his back, the blade dwarfing him, but not slowing him. He thinks that it was pointless to bring it. The Custodian is dead, and the target stands on the bridge beneath him. He is satisfied by this – in his centuries of work, he has learnt that chance is a powerful force that you follow rather than question.

'Do you have the target?' He speaks the words sub-vocally, but the Vindicare Kestra hears it clear in her ear. She is watching the exchange on the bridge through the sight of her rifle. Crouched half a mile above the bridge amongst cobwebbed statues, she is a shadow amongst shadows. The round loaded into her gun's breech is a murderous thing that no armour or energy field will stop. Her range is set. Her muscles aligned. Her whole being focused on the target.

'I have him,' she says. 'The others?'

'An irrelevance. Remove the primary target. The Custodians can deal with these other interlopers.'

'As you wish…'

The image in the gunsight fills Kestra's eye. She can feel the kill balanced in the motion of her finger.

The bolt roars out of the dark and rips the Assassin's gun arm from her torso. She twists, fast. Muscles and nerves sculpted by gene and bio-grafts mean that she does not feel her wound. Blood is pouring down her side from the remains of her shoulder. She has a pistol in her hand, and her eyes find the armoured figure crouched a quarter of a mile above her.

Hunters and the hunted… I said I was not done, didn't I?

The warrior that took the shot is Zhorn. My Legion brother has waited, his armour powered down to immobility, body heat masked, heartbeat barely a murmur. With his shot he has revealed himself to the Vindicare. So, now she is going to kill him. A kill shot against a Space Marine, from a quarter of a mile away, with a pistol, as lifeblood is pouring from you… It should not be possible. But the Assassins are made to make such feats real.

Kestra shoots at the same moment as Zhorn. The round from her pistol tears open his helm and skull. The bolt-round from his gun punches her back into the air above the drop below and explodes her into a spray of bone.

* * *

'What–' Mordachi's head twitches up at the sound of gunshots, and the figure on the bridge comes at him. Mordachi should have felt the blow coming, should have sensed the killing impulse ripple the future, should have heard the snarl in the hooded figure's thoughts. But all his mind can hear is the wail of the dead, and the roar of the Golden Throne. Instinct and superhuman speed save his life.

Mordachi twitches aside as the first blow falls. He realises then that it is not me. It's Korlael, of course. Righteous and deadly, my truest brother. Energised steel shears ceramite from Mordachi's right shoulder. Then his own sword is blazing with the light of his mind and he is cutting back, and Korlael is meeting the blows.

'It's not him. Nariel–' shouts Mordachi into the vox.

But Nariel does not hear the shout. At that moment my remaining Fallen brothers open up. They have been waiting.

Bolt-rounds explode into Nariel and the Dark Angels. Detonations chew the chasm wall where they made their firing positions. Balconies and statue plinths shatter and tumble downwards. A tongue of stone hinges down from the wall above them. Two of the Dark Angels fall with it, toppling into the dark to be crushed at the end of their fall. The third leaps back in time, hands and feet find purchase for long enough for him to swing up into a niche above. Fire explodes through the statue he crouches behind. Shock waves slam through his armour. Red warning runes paint his sight. Then he too is falling, down and down into the dark.

From his eyrie above the bridge, Cradus hisses an oath and turns away from the gunfire and kin-slaughter. This is not a fight of Assassins now, and he knows that they have lost both an operative and the chance of taking my life. Still, even with that loss of face and resource, he still has the sword. That is a comfort of sorts. He will leave now and take it back to the vaults of the Assassinorum. The old murderer swings down between the dust-covered statues of saints and dead warriors that line the clifflike wall above the bridge. The shadows, ever his home and his refuge, wrap around him. He curses himself for ever having let Hekkarron persuade them to join in this hunt of fools. He lands, catlike, on a stone walkway.

I am waiting for him.

He realises I am there just before my bolt shell rips his body in half.

He is dead before the plasma shot burns the head from his corpse, but with his kind it pays to be thorough. It is no small or easy thing to kill an Imperial Assassin, much less one as experienced as Cradus. But I have done this before.

I walk to the corpse. The sword is still strapped to the remains. The sheath is burnt and torn by shrapnel, but the blade within is untouched. It will take more than plasma or the touch of a bolt-round to mark its metal.

I holster my guns and lift the blade. I have borne it for so long… How much longer must it be mine? Too long, and not long enough. I bow my head and close my eyes. Then I sling it across my shoulders.

I have the sword again. Did I plan that? It seems like something that cannot be planned, don't you think? And it's a strange plan that returns something to you that you only recently lost.

I shrug the pistols into my hands again. I am angry. When I reach the bridge Korlael will be dying. I am sorry for that. I am sorry for everything that has happened and will happen.

So why did I choose to come here? Why did I do this?

What made you think I had a choice?

SEVENTEEN

Hekkarron's Mindscape

Hekkarron is lying on rough black stone beneath a red sky. The spray of breaking waves touches his face. He rises to his feet. He is clothed in gold and tongues of flame. He looks around. The sky swirls with clouds lit by fire and curdled by smoke. The sea extends from the rock he stands on to a black horizon. Its surface heaves, black water rolls into brief valleys of shadow and peaks of obsidian. He can smell salt, and something else, something metallic that he feels he should recognise. A wave rolls from the sea and breaks over the rock. The water is cold on his skin. He raises a hand to touch it as it runs down his face.

'It is not real,' rasps a voice.

Hekkarron whirls. A tall figure, wrapped in black, stands three paces from him. The cloth of its robes leeches the light from the air. Its face is a yellow skull. It is the image of Theta, the Voice of the Court of Assassins.

'None of this is real.'

'A death dream,' says Hekkarron to himself.

'A dream…' says the figure, the word as much an echo as an agreement.

Hekkarron turns to them. 'And you are a phantom of my mind,' he says.

'A phantom…'

The image tilts its head but does not bow or speak. It watches. Hekkarron turns in a full circle again, measuring sea and rock and sky with a look.

'I cannot be here. If there is breath left to me I must draw it in the waking world. I must rise. I must go to–'

'You must remain, Hekkarron-Ageon-Cataphra-Alupunra-Tambrione,' interrupts the figure.

Hekkarron flinches at the sound of his full name. He narrows his gaze at the figure's skull face. The salt-heavy wind whips the ragged folds of their cloak.

'This place is false. My duty waits in the real world.'

'This is not falsehood. It is a dream.'

Hekkarron does not move. He is a thing of great intelligence, but intelligence is not knowledge, and in all the years that he can remember he has never dreamed. His kind have not dreamed since the Emperor took His place on the Golden Throne. Hekkarron has read of dreams, listened to accounts of them and knows enough that he can stitch together an idea of their texture and dimension. But an idea is not the thing itself. So Hekkarron does not know that the phantom before him is lying. This is no dream.

'I need to wake. I need to rise,' he says.

'You need to see…'

'I must–'

'See.'

And the dream around the figure of Theta changes. The sea shrinks from the island of black stone as it thrusts into the sky. Hekkarron looks up as a bolt of lightning strikes down from the cloud. White light explodes around him. Pain floods through him.

'You must see...'

The blinding light vanishes. All around Hekkarron are stars. Black infinity stretches beyond jewels of fire. For an instant it is still, serene. Then a crack unfolds amongst the pinprick illuminations. Nausea light spills out, flowing like blood from a bullet wound.

'The Eye of Terror...' breathes Hekkarron. The arc of stars turns like a spinning blade. Hekkarron cannot move or speak and cannot close his eyes. Crimson pours into the dark, a great bleeding smile of fire across the disc of the galaxy. On and on the red light pours, ever outwards, eating the stars until there is nothing but crimson and the buzzing of its laughter in Hekkarron's ears.

Then silence. The red heavens are gone. Now, where there were stars stands a city. Towers and domes rise around Hekkarron, mountains of stone and statuary. Dust blows through their broken doors and shattered windows. Bones lie in the shadows. Hekkarron stares. He knows this place, knows it as only one who has lived decades walking its ways can. It is not the same, it is like a dream of the true place, a fading memory of something that has not happened yet.

'A dream...' he says.

'An inevitability,' says Theta. The image of the Voice of the Abyss is standing behind him when he turns. The dust wind stirs the black wrappings of her robes.

'No, this cannot happen. It will not happen.'

'Hopes and dreams are how we got here,' says the image of Theta. 'The fight to prevent this future began millennia on millennia ago. It has not been won.'

Hekkarron turns away and takes a step forward. He does not know why but he has to see if what he fears is in this nightmare too. Heaped ash and dust drag at his legs as he moves. The powder is the colour of rust.

'Others have seen this place and walked its highways and halls,' says the Voice behind him. 'As the age darkens, more and more come here. And see what shall be. It has a name... Do you know it?'

Hekkarron knows. He has read the reports of inquisitors. He has reviewed the sealed archive material. He has listened to the recordings of so-called heretics and saints. He knows where he is, but he speaks the words reluctantly.

'The Desolate City.'

'Just so.'

The image of the Voice of the Abyss bows its head in assent. Hekkarron moves on, wading down a canyon made by half-collapsed buildings. The image of Theta follows him.

I have never seen the Desolate City, though I have heard it spoken of by the broken and the all-too-sane. It is a shadow place that exists where dream and vision and nightmare meet. It is both real and not, an un-place, a destination not yet arrived at. I am glad I have not seen it. The truth is not a kind thing to see made real.

'Please...'

Hekkarron hears the voice on the wind. His head comes up. He pauses. 'That was a voice.'

'Just so,' says Theta.

'Please...'

Still Hekkarron does not move. He does not want to. At the deepest level of his being he does not want to. After a long moment, he forces his legs to move through the dust. The city folds around him as he walks. Skulls grin at him from mounds of bones. The dust tastes like rust on his tongue. Like iron. Like blood.

He turns a corner, and there it is. It makes him stop. Behind him the image of the Voice of the Abyss lets out a breath that sounds like a chuckle.

'You see...'

And see he does. For there on a seat of stone sits a man. The hair and skin that wrap His skull are pale. The purple of His robes is ragged. The hands that grip the arms of the Throne are spiders of bone. The Throne itself is simple, a plain seat without adornment. It sits at the centre of a cracked plaza. Both seat and man are small, human-sized to Hekkarron's eyes, but somehow they also fill the world by simply being. That one figure on a simple stone chair is the greatest and most terrible thing Hekkarron has ever seen.

He begins to kneel, though if in reverence or in shock, even he does not know.

'It... cannot be...' he murmurs.

'It is and shall be.'

The dust wind is blowing strong now. Folds of red and ochre swallow the towers and buildings. The figure on the Throne turns its head then. A slow movement. The eyes inside the sockets are hard and black. Hekkarron tries to turn his gaze from them, but cannot, and then the figure on the Throne is lifting a withered hand, and reaching out.

'Please...' It is a dying word, a word of pain, and life vanishing beyond eternity.

The distance between them collapses, and the withered hand

grasps Hekkarron's even as the Custodian reaches in response. The fingers turn to dust in Hekkarron's grasp. The image of the Desolate City and the old figure on the Throne dissolves into the dust clouds. Only he and the figure in black remain. The sockets of its skull mask meet Hekkarron's eyes.

'Do you see?'

Hekkarron nods.

'Yes.' He knows now that he is both dreaming and not. He knows that he has not understood until now. 'The city is what the Imperium will become, what the Emperor will become, what everything will become.'

The figure of Theta turns its head as though looking at something only it can see.

'Is it inevitable?'

'You think I can give you an answer?' asks the image of Theta. 'That I can give you truth?'

'Yes,' says Hekkarron.

'Then you know who I am,' says the figure in the skull mask.

'Yes,' says Hekkarron.

Ah… Do you know? Do you suspect? Do you guess what is happening here? This is the moment when we should look away, too, where the answer should remain unsaid, where the mystery should be preserved. Is this divine intervention the delusion of a dying warrior? Best that we don't know. Best that we can dream it is both truth or falsity… Who is the image of Theta? Was the city and the figure on the Throne a dying Emperor or a lie created by the warp and the fears of mankind? Is this real or a lie?

Well… that would be a secret. I will give you the truth instead. Watch, and listen.

'There is something you must know,' says the figure that looks like Theta but is not. 'There is something that you must do.'

And the figure in black with a death's head tells Hekkarron what he must do. And for a moment, for a beautiful golden moment, everything that has happened or might happen makes sense. Hekkarron bows his head.

'You wish to know more,' says the figure. Hekkarron shakes his head, but the skull-faced spectre was not asking a question. 'You wish to know more. You wish to know why.'

'I do,' says Hekkarron at last.

The eyes of the skull mask look back at him. Then the figure in black turns and raises an arm, and the dream opens like a door.

And Hekkarron sees. He sees.

Perhaps he sees a warrior in black armour drawing a sword and plunging it into a figure on a golden throne. Perhaps he sees a figure robed like a vagabond of night kneeling and raising the sword of his father, head bowed in penance and pleading. Perhaps he sees light blazing out into the night, on and on through the stars. Perhaps he sees those same stars fade and then gutter. Perhaps he sees this and more. I do not know. I do not wish to know.

'Hekkarron!'

Then he hears the shout. It is Ancia's voice.

'Hekkarron!'

He is falling again, out of visions of fire and gold, down and down through black to the cold stone of a floor where blood fills his mouth and pools beneath him.

The Path of Martyrs

'Hekkarron!' calls Ancia. She is crouched above him. His helm lies beside him, and her fingers are clamped on his scalp. Frost cakes her hands. Smoke and the scent of ozone rise through the air.

'I…' gasps Hekkarron. 'I saw…'

'You live, everything else is secondary.'

'It was no dream. I saw–'

'I know. I was there at the end, in your thoughts.'

Hekkarron and Ancia lock eyes.

'It was…'

'A vision. And visions are not truth. Take it from me.'

'It was Him.'

Ancia's face is set. 'Your wounds… The veil of death brings things out of the dark, even in minds like yours.'

Unspoken truths circle in the silence that follows. Hekkarron pushes himself up. Blood and shards of cracked armour fall from him. His face is a mass of clotted blood. One eye is closed beneath a flap of chewed meat. Just because they are made with divinity woven into their flesh does not mean they don't bleed.

'Your wounds,' says Ancia. 'You should not–'

'What can you see of the future now?' Hekkarron asks.

Ancia opens her mouth to argue, then stops. Her eyes move over the black, gold and bloody ruin of Hekkarron. He should not be standing. He should not be able to stand. It is an image of the duty that the Emperor demands of His subjects and the price they pay for loyalty.

'I will look,' says Ancia.

She places her hands on the bloody stones of the floor beside her. Her mind opens to the flow of the warp. Globules of blood pull from the floor as she moves. Her eyes have become the white of dirty ice. She is seeing now, or trying to. Before her the ghosts of futures rise and fall, all insubstantial, all crumbling.

'I can see no clear path from here. Only disasters near or far. The Emperor dead, the Imperium aflame… but… I cannot see which path is which, or if it is many paths.'

Hekkarron nods and picks up his guardian spear and helm. He turns and begins to move towards the open gate into the Inner Sanctum.

'What are you going to do?' she asks.

'What I must.'

EIGHTEEN

Inner Sanctum, Bridge of Ascension

Mordachi meets Korlael's blade again. Sparks and lightning rise from the touch of the swords. Spinning steel and lightning, razor edges and blurred movement. It is a fight of complete lethality. The Librarian's mind, ever his truest weapon, is reeling. The death cries from the Golden Throne are deafening. He knows he is going to lose, knows he is going to die to the blade of the Fallen kin whose name he does not even know.

Korlael's blow hammers Mordachi's sword down. The Librarian of the Dark Angels counters the thrust that comes after, but only just. He is going back across the bridge. Around and above them, gunfire howls between the cliff walls. My brother can feel the close of this fight coming. The weakness of the Dark Angel is to be expected, but it is not what will kill the warrior. It is errors. Hundreds of points of nuance in cut and thrust, in the switch of grip and the whisper of edge, each of them imperceptible to even a Space Marine. They are the difference bred by survival and lifetimes lived by the sword. Small. Marginal. But their accumulation is enough to tip the scales of life.

'You are false sons of the Lion!' Mordachi snarls his words as Korlael strikes again, heavy then swift, that switch in rhythm like a breath of air. The force sword in Mordachi's grasp moves and meets the blows. The sliver of Mordachi's will within the blade is driving it now as much as muscle. Mordachi can hear the howls of the dead clearly. Can almost hear the words they shriek. They are calling to him, he thinks.

'You betrayed your brothers,' says Korlael.

Korlael strikes once, twice, three times, each swing a hammer blow that drives Mordachi back. He tries to return the strike, but Korlael has his measure, and scythes his sword low. Lightning-sheathed steel cuts into Mordachi's left thigh. Splinters of ceramite and droplets of burning blood scatter as he drops to one knee.

'Mordachi!' The shout is from Nariel. The sergeant is running across the bridge to Mordachi's side.

Korlael spins his sword up faster than Mordachi can follow. It is a killing blow now. Point down, the strike of an executioner. Mordachi has time to look up into the eyes of Korlael. He feels his killer's pity.

'Korlael,' says Mordachi.

It is the name that Mordachi saw in the eyes of his killer. It is enough to stop the down thrust of the blade for an instant. An instant where Mordachi thrusts up with his own blade. The psychic fire sheathing the sword parts the ceramite over Korlael's ribs. Steel punches up into my brother's chest. Sharp edges pierce lungs and hearts.

Korlael gasps blood. For an instant he hangs on the blade.

He still has his own weapon raised. Then Mordachi sends his will through the sword. Psychic fire rips through Korlael. Flesh blasts to ash, armour shatters.

Mordachi rises from the ground. He looks at the wall of the canyon. His teeth are bared inside his helm. He is a controlled soul, but in this moment he feels rage. He feels that he has lost something – honour, maybe. He sees the area of the canyon wall where the last few of my brothers are training their weapons at the bridge. He levels his sword, and the rage and shame within him burn from its point. Flames leap through the air, white-hot. Stone flashes to slag. The beam of psychic fire expands, slicing along the building front. A wash of melting stone and superheated gas rolls out. There are bodies in that glow. My Fallen brothers, the swiftness of their gene-forged flesh not swift enough, nor their armour proof against the flames. They loathed me, or feared me, or were fools to follow me. I will not mourn them. But I will avenge them.

The line of fire vanishes. Mordachi is shivering, sweat is pouring from his flesh inside his armour. The pain in his head is almost blinding. He pulls his helmet off. The screaming that only he can hear is so, so loud in the silence of his skull.

'Brother-Librarian?' Nariel is at Mordachi's side, gun up and looking for targets. He alone has survived from those that came on this doomed mission. A good warrior, Nariel, loyal, strong, and true to his oaths. He jerks his head at Korlael's remains. 'Was it him? Was it Cypher?'

Mordachi is forcing the shiver from his hands, blinking as black spots roll across his sight. Nariel is alert, eyes fixed on his surroundings, ready.

'I...' gasps Mordachi. 'Nariel... We must...'

'Brother?' Nariel glances at Mordachi. A quick glance, just a sliver of time in which his gaze goes from the world around him to the Librarian.

Nariel's helm and head blow to smoke and ash in a flash of light. His body drops to the floor.

I walk out onto the bridge, pistols in my hands, my hands at my sides. Heat curls from my plasma pistol.

Mordachi straightens, his sight clearing as he sees me.

'You…' he breathes. He knows it is me, even though we have never met before.

I stop. A span of twelve paces separates us. Somewhere, rushing closer, are the forces that remain to guard this inner part of the Palace. Soon there will be Custodians, and Knights and auxilia will be swarming over this bridge. But they are not here yet. First there must be this moment, where Mordachi summons his strength and I wait in stillness.

'Ask,' I say at last. 'You want to know. So ask.'

Mordachi shakes his head, but he wants to know the truth.

'Why did you come here?' he asks.

'Because someone had to.'

'You die here, Fallen One. I alone remain, but I will be enough. You slaughtered my brothers,' he says. He is genuinely angry. 'You-'

'That is not what you are here to say.' My words cut through him. Duty and training take the place of outrage.

'Submit,' he says. 'Plead for forgiveness, and you shall be granted absolution.'

'Yes…' I nod, slowly. 'That was it.' The wind fills the moment that follows. 'When you are ready, brother.'

The wind breathes… It is beautiful here. Everything is balanced on this instant. The future, the meaning of the past: all of it is here in the smell of smoke and the–

A flash of fire. Two bolt-rounds kissing the air with flame as they fly…

Lightning flash. The reek of ozone…

Thunder…

The shots I fired never reach their target. In the time that it took them to cross half the distance between us, Mordachi has bound me with chains of lightning.

'You will not go back to the chains that wait for you in our dungeons,' says Mordachi. 'You shall burn here, in the sight of the Throne you turned from.'

'Do… you…' I ask with effort, 'want the truth?'

'You are a serpent.'

'Look into my thoughts. The truth is there. It is my confession.'

He should know better, shouldn't he? You don't ask for the truth, because if it does exist it will only bring you sorrow. Mordachi, though, like all of the newly bred sons of our father, can't help but want what he should refuse.

'Show me,' he says.

And…

And here *you* are with me. And I have told you and shown you the truth.

I am standing now, free of the chains of lightning that held me. I am walking closer. My gun is rising. Nothing is stopping me. The will to do it is not in you. It is here listening. Waiting for what comes next.

I am here. A last stranger, and the end of a tale.

You should not have looked. Should not have wanted to know the truth. It has killed you in the end. Wanting to know what should not be known has left your sword frozen in your hand while your mind scrolls through all I have told you. In these last seconds you are going to wonder if any of it was true at all. You are going to wonder whose story this was if it wasn't mine and wasn't yours. I cannot release you from that burden.

You see, everyone asks for the truth…

But what you should ask for are secrets.

I lower the gun. The corpse of Epistolary Mordachi lies at my feet. Blood is spreading across the stones of the bridge. I look up to where ash and debris are still dribbling from the wounds in the walls either side of the chasm. More dead lie amongst the rubble and down in the dark of the abyss beneath. I alone now remain. A false wind stirs the robes that hang over my armour. The great sword hanging at my back shifts as I holster my pistols.

I turn towards the far end of the bridge.

'You may pass no further,' says Hekkarron. The Warden of the Dark Cells stands at the end of the bridge. His guardian spear is upright in his hand. His armour is cracked and streaked with blood, his face a mass of clotting wounds. But he is unmoving, poised, a sentinel of broken gold. I look at the Custodian. Our gazes lock.

'I knew you would be here,' I say.

'You could not have known that,' he replies.

'Someone like you had to be here.'

Hekkarron gives the smallest of nods. 'And here I am.'

I shake my head. 'I have given everything to be here,' I say, and I can hear the weariness in my voice.

'Yes,' says Hekkarron, 'but I have a duty I must perform, and you cannot pass.'

'Then all must be as it must.'

I remain still, not the stillness of readiness, but of consideration. I am wondering if I should kill Hekkarron. He is wondering if I can.

'I know where you are going,' says Hekkarron, 'and perhaps why.'

'You cannot know that,' I say.

'You asked me once if I wanted to know a secret, now I tell you that I have something that I must say to you, and that you must hear.'

'I will pass here,' I say. 'You are bound to try and stop me. One will live. That is the only answer that matters. What can be said that could change anything?'

'Not yet,' says Hekkarron.

I blink once. Hekkarron does not move but waits as the beat of his heart passes in the silence.

'Is that a message?'

Hekkarron tilts his head. 'The choice is yours, heed what has been said and go from this place, or continue.'

'You are a gaoler and a Custodian, you cannot let me go.'

'I have my duty, and I serve one thing above all else.'

Slowly I nod, and then, with the weight of what I still must bear pressing down on me, I bow my head.

'Not yet…' I repeat to myself.

My weight shifts to take a step. Hekkarron grips his spear.

Then I turn and begin to walk back along the bridge. I stop after five paces, half turn, the hood of my robe pulling a shadow across my face.

'It will be difficult to leave this place,' I say.

'I am sure you will find a path,' says Hekkarron. 'You have come this far. What is one more step?'

I pause for a second then continue walking, the great sword hung across my back. Hekkarron watches me until I am out of sight in the shadows on the other side of the bridge. He feels the cold coming over him slowly. Death, long staved off, now flows through blood and sinew. His muscles begin to lock. His sight dims slowly. Inside his armour, the wounds that killed him hours ago weep the last drops of blood with a final beat of his heart.

CLOSURE

Are you there? Are you listening? This is where we are going to end. On the edge of the place where a throne sits and the screams of the dead pull frost from the air, a place guarded by gilded demigods, a place where a bridge spans an abyss, and where two of those guardians stand. One is called Cambyses, the other Drayth. They are warriors, they are bodyguards, they are killers. While they talk, they think they go unheard...

Listen...

'The Doomscryer Ancia remembers nothing of what occurred. Not the vision that she reported to Warden Hekkarron, not her actions at this side, nothing...'

'That is concerning. Security access logs and pict monitors all confirm that she both started the actions taken by Warden Hekkarron by bringing him a foresight and personally aided him after that.'

'Indeed. Her mind is being assayed, but her lack of recall and her actions are true.'

'Could she have been possessed?'

'The subtlety of daemons is never to be underestimated, but probability and evidence point against it.'

'Control by an external psychic force, then?'

'That remains a possibility, but to control the actions and edit the thoughts of a Doomscryer within the Palace, in the presence of a Custodian... that would imply a psychic might that is... concerning.'

'As are the actions of Warden Hekkarron before he died. The prisoners that broke from the Dark Cells almost reached the Throne Room. The one marked as Cypher stood on this spot, and Hekkarron let him go.'

'That is impossible. One of our kind cannot act to endanger the Principal. Cypher was a threat. To let him live and walk free was therefore to aid an action against the Principal.'

'Indeed. It is impossible. Unless he was ordered to let the one called Cypher go free.'

'And none may order us so. We may not act against His will or interest...'

'So Hekkarron's actions cannot have been against His will, and therefore...'

They are silent then, disturbed by questions and implications. Poor souls. They are making a mistake.

'We shall hunt the fugitive and we shall find them. We cannot let this go...'

'Unanswered? No. We cannot.'

The two leave the bridge, and the ghost wind howls through the space where they stood. They shall hunt their quarry across the stars and into the lost night of the Imperium. They shall think they hunt because they want to protect their master and Emperor. They think that one who came so close to breaking their guard cannot be allowed to come so close again. There is truth in that, but the real reason they will hunt is not because of what happened but because they have become infected with the need to answer the questions that buzz in their minds. And by now, you know what that means. They want something that you should not ask for and will not set you free.

You understand that. You have listened. You know.

Now, though, this must end, as all things must. As all stories must, whether true or not…

Was it true?

Well…

Do you want to know a secret?

ABOUT THE AUTHOR

John French is the author of several Horus Heresy stories including the novels *The Solar War, Mortis, Praetorian of Dorn, Tallarn, Slaves to Darkness* and *Sigismund: The Eternal Crusader,* the novella *The Crimson Fist,* and the audio dramas *Dark Compliance, Templar* and *Warmaster.* For Warhammer 40,000 he has written *Resurrection, Incarnation* and *Divination* for The Horusian Wars and three tie-in audio dramas – the Scribe Award-winning *Agent of the Throne: Blood and Lies,* as well as *Agent of the Throne: Truth and Dreams* and *Agent of the Throne: Ashes and Oaths.* John has also written the Ahriman series, the Age of Sigmar novel *The Hollow King* and many short stories.

THE LION: SON OF THE FOREST
by Mike Brooks

After ten thousand years, Lion El'Jonson has returned. But now, he finds himself trapped in the nightmare of Imperium Nihilus, where the dying embers of humanity are threatened on all sides by the darkness.

An extract from
The Lion: Son of The Forest
by Mike Brooks

The river sings silver notes: a perpetual, chaotic babble in which a fantastically complex melody seems to hang, tantalising, just out of reach of the listener. He could spend eternity here trying to find the heart of it, without ever succeeding, yet still not consider the time wasted. The sound of water over stone, the interplay of energy and matter, creates a quiet symphony that is both unremarkable and unique. He does not know how long he has been here, just listening.

Nor, he realises, does he know where *here* is.

The listener becomes aware of himself in stages, like a sleeper passing from the deepest, darkest depths of slumber, through the shallows of semi-consciousness where thought swirls in confusing eddies, and then into the light. First comes the realisation that he is not the song of the river; that he is in fact separate from it, and listening to it. Then sensation dawns, and he realises he is sitting on the river's bank. If there is a sun, or suns, then he cannot see them through the branches of the trees overhead and the mist that hangs heavily in the air, but there is still light enough for him to make out his surroundings.

The trees are massive, and mighty, with great trunks that could not be fully encircled by one, two, perhaps even half a dozen people's outstretched arms. Their rough, cracked bark pockmarks them with shadows, as though the trees themselves are camouflaged. The ground beneath their branches is fought over by tough shrubs: sturdy, twisted, thorny things strangling each other in the contest for space and light, like children unheeded at the feet of adults. The earth in which they grow is dark and rich, and when the listener digs his fingers into it, it smells of life, and death, and other things besides. It is a familiar smell, although he cannot say from where, or why.

His fingers, he realises as they penetrate the ground, are armoured. His whole body is armoured, in fact, encased in a great suit of black plates with the faintest hint of dark green. This is a familiar sensation, too. The armour feels like a part of him – an extension, as natural as the shell of any crustacean that might lurk in the nooks and crannies of the river in front of him. He leans forward and peers down into the still water next to the bank, sheltered from the main flow by an outcropping just upstream. It becomes an almost perfect mirror surface, as smooth as a dream.

The listener does not recognise the face that looks back at him. It is deeply lined, as though a world of cares and worries has washed over it like the river water, scoring the marks of their passage into the skin. His hair is pale, streaked with blond here and there, but otherwise fading into grey and white. The lower part of his face is obscured by a thick, full beard and moustache, leaving only the lips bare; it is a distrustful mouth, one more likely to turn downwards in disapproval than quirk upwards in a smile.

He raises one hand, the fingers still smeared with dirt, before his face. The reflection does the same. This is surely his face, but the sight sparks no memory. He does not know who he is, and he does not know where he is, for all that it feels familiar.

That being the case, there seems little point in remaining here.

The listener gets to his feet, then hesitates. He cannot explain to himself why he should move, given the song of the river is so beautiful. However, the realisation of his lack of knowledge has opened something inside him, a hunger which was not there before. He will not be satisfied until he has answers.

Still, the river's song calls to him. He decides to walk along the bank, following the flow of the water and listening to it as he goes, and since he does not know where he is, one direction is as good as the other. There is a helmet on the bank, next to where he was sitting. It is the same colour as his armour, with vertical slits across the mouth, like firing slits in a wall. He picks it up, and clamps it to his waist with a movement that feels instinctual.

He does not know for how long he walks. Time is surely passing, in that one moment slips into another, and he can remember ones that came before and consider the concept of ones yet to come, but there is nothing to mark it. The light neither increases nor decreases, instead remaining an almost spectral presence which illuminates without revealing its source. Shadows lurk, but there is no indication as to what casts them. The walker is unperturbed. His eyes can pierce those shadows, just as he can smell foliage, and he can hear the river. There is no soughing of wind in the branches, for the air is still, but the moist air carries the faint hooting, hollering calls of animals of some kind, somewhere in the distance.

The river's course begins to flatten and widen. The walker follows it around a bend, then comes to a halt in shock.

On the far bank stands a building.

It is built of cut and dressed stone, a dark blue-grey rock in which brighter specks glitter. It is not immense – the surrounding trees tower over it – but it is solid. It is a castle of some kind, a fortress, intended to keep the unwanted out and whatever people and treasures lie within safe from harm. It is neither new and pristine, nor ancient and weathered. It looks as though it has always stood here, and always shall. And on the wide, calm water in front of it sits a boat.

It is small, wooden, and unpainted. It is large enough for one person, and indeed one person is sitting in it. The walker's eyes can make him out, even at distance. He is old, and not old in the same way as the walker's face is. Time has not lined his features, it has ravaged them. His cheeks are sunken, his limbs are wasted; skin that was once clearly a rich chestnut now has an ashen patina, and his long hair is lifeless, dull grey, and matted. However, that grey head supports a crown: little more than a circlet of gold, but a crown nonetheless.

In his hands, swollen of knuckle and weak of grip, he holds a rod. The line is already cast into the water. Now he sits, hunched over as though in pain, a small, ancient figure in a small, simple boat.

The walker does not stop to wonder why a king would be fishing in such a manner. He is aware of the context of such things, but he does not know from where, and they do not matter to him. Here is someone who might have some answers for him.

'Greetings!' he calls. His voice is strong, rich and deep,

although rough around the edges from age or disuse, or both. It carries across the water. The old king in the boat blinks, and when his eyes open again, they are looking at the walker.

'What is this place?' the walker demands.

The old king blinks again. When his eyes open this time, they are focused on the water once more. It is as though the walker is not there at all, a dismissal of minimal effort.

The walker discovers that he is not used to being ignored, and nor does he appreciate it. He steps into the water, intending to wade across the river so the king cannot so easily dismiss him. He is unconcerned about the current: he is strong of limb, and knows without knowing that his armour is waterproof, and that should he don his helmet he will be able to breathe even if he is submerged.

He has only gone a few steps, in up to his knees, when he realises there are shadows in the water: large shadows that circle the small boat, around and around. They do not bite on the line, and nor do they capsize the craft in which the fisher sits, but either could be disastrous.

Moreover, the walker realises, the king is wounded. The walker cannot see the wound, but he can smell the blood. A rich, copperish tang tickles his nose. It is not a smell that delights him, but neither does he find it repulsive. It is simply a scent, one that he is able to parse and understand. The king is bleeding into the water, drip by drip. Perhaps that is what has drawn the shadows to this place. Perhaps they would have been here anyway.

Some of the shadows start to peel away, and head towards the walker.

The walker is not a being to whom fear comes naturally, but nor is he unfamiliar with the concept of danger. The shadows in the water are unknown to him, and move like predators.

+Come back to the bank.+

The walker whirls. A small figure stands on the land, swathed in robes of dark green, so that it nearly blends into the background against which it stands. It is the size of a child, perhaps, but the walker knows it to be something else.

It is a Watcher in the Dark.

+Come back to the bank,+ the Watcher repeats. Although its communication can hardly be called a voice – there is no sound, merely a sensation inside the walker's head that imparts meaning – it feels increasingly urgent nonetheless. The walker realises that he is not normally one to turn away from a challenge, but nor is he willing to ignore a Watcher in the Dark. It feels like a link, a connection to what came before, to what he should be able to remember.

He wades back, and steps up onto the bank. The approaching shadows hesitate for a moment, then circle away towards the king in his boat.

+They would destroy you,+ the Watcher says. The walker understands that it is talking about the shadows. There are layers to the feelings in his head now, feelings that are the mental aftertaste of the Watcher's communication. Disgust lurks there, but also fear.

'Where is this place?' the walker asks.

+Home.+

The walker waits, but nothing else is forthcoming. Moreover, he understands that there will not be. So far as the Watcher is concerned, that is not simply all the information that is required, but all that is available to give.

He looks out over the water, towards the king. The old man still sits hunched over, rod in his hands, blood leaking from his wounds one drip at a time.

'Why does he ignore me?'

+You did not ask the correct question.+

The walker looks around. The shadows in the water are still there, so it seems foolish to try to cross. However, he has seen no bridge over the river, nor another boat. He has no tools with which to build such a craft from the trees around him, and the knowledge of how to do so does not come easily to his mind. He is not like some of his brothers, for whom creation is natural...

His brothers. Who are his brothers?

Shapes flit through his mind, as ephemeral as smoke in a storm. He cannot get a grip, cannot wrestle them into anything that makes sense, or anything onto which his reaching mind can latch. The peace brought about by the song of the river is gone, and in its place is uncertainty and frustration. Nonetheless, the walker would not return to his former state. To knowingly welcome ignorance is not his way.

He catches a glimpse of something pale, a long way off through the trees, but on his side of the river. He begins to walk towards it, leaving the river behind him – he can always find it again, he knows its song – and making his way through the undergrowth. The plants are thick and verdant, but he is strong and sure. He ducks under spines, slaps aside strangling tendrils reaching out for anything that passes, and avoids breaking the twigs, which would leak sap so corrosive it might damage even his armour.

He does not wonder how he knows these things. The Watcher said that this was home.

The Watcher itself has been left behind, but it keeps reappearing, stepping out of the edge of shadows. It says nothing; not until the walker passes through a thicket of thorns and finally gets a clearer view of what he had seen.

It is a building, or at least the roof of one; that is all he can see from here. It is a dome of beautiful pale stone, supported by pillars. Whereas before he had been finding his own route through the forest, now there is a clear path ahead, a route of short grass hemmed in on either side by bushes and tree trunks. It curves away, rather than arrowing straight towards the pale building, but the walker knows that is where it leads.

+Do not take that path,+ the Watcher cautions him. +You are not yet strong enough.+

The walker looks down at this tiny creature, barely knee-high to him, then breathes deeply and rolls his shoulders within his armour. He presumes he had a youth, given he now looks old. Perhaps he was stronger then. Nonetheless, his body does not feel feeble.

+That is not the strength you will need.+

The walker narrows his eyes. 'You caution me against anything that might help me make sense of my situation. What would you have me do instead?'

+Follow your nature.+

The walker breathes in again, ready to snap an answer, for he finds he is just as ill-disposed towards being denied as he is to being ignored. However, he pauses, then sniffs.

He sniffs again.

Something is amiss.

He is surrounded by the deep, rich scent of the forest, which smells of both life and death. However, now his nose detects something else: a rancid undercurrent, something that is not merely rot or decay – for these are natural odours – but far worse, far more jarring.

Corruption.

This is something wrong, something twisted. It is something that should not be here: something that should not, in fact, exist at all.

The walker knows what he must do. He must follow his nature.

The hunter steps forward, and starts to run in pursuit of his quarry.